OLD WOUNDS

Liam asked, "Rambling Jim, do you know the cause of the difficulties between our uncle and Bret Ellison?"

"It goes way back. It involved a woman, I believe. The woman Ellison married later on."

"Maybe Patrick and Ellison were after the same woman, and that caused the resentment."

"All Ellison would say on it was that he holds Patrick Carrigan responsible for the biggest loss in his life. And that he'll never forgive what was done."

"Biggest loss . . . money? Land?"

"I can only think he means his woman. The loss of his wife."

"How would Patrick be responsible for that?"

"I don't know. But if you could find out that answer, you might then understand what lies behind the war at Fire Creek."

Also by Cameron Judd

SHOOTOUT IN DODGE CITY

REVENGE ON SHADOW TRAIL

CAMERON JUDD

WAR AT FIRE CREEK

POCKET STAR BOOKS

NEW YORK   LONDON   TORONTO   SYDNEY

An *Original* Publication of POCKET BOOKS

A Pocket Star Book published by
POCKET BOOKS, a division of Simon & Schuster, Inc.
1230 Avenue of the Americas, New York, NY 10020

ISBN: 0-7434-5710-2

First Pocket Books printing August 2004

10   9   8   7   6   5   4   3   2   1

POCKET STAR BOOKS and colophon are registered trademarks of Simon & Schuster, Inc.

Cover design by Patrick Kang
Photo courtesy of author

Manufactured in the United States of America

For information regarding special discounts for bulk purchases, please contact Simon & Schuster Special Sales at 1-800-456-6798 or business@simonandschuster.com.

WAR AT FIRE CREEK

CHAPTER ONE

"Pardon me . . . 'scuse me, please," said Liam Carrigan as he trod on toes and kicked ankles while working his way toward a seat in the dark show hall. Joseph, his brother, had entered earlier and already was in place on down the row, with a seat saved for Liam at his left side.

Liam plopped into his chair, looked around, and side-whispered loudly to Joseph: "Why the hell is it so dark? The show ain't even started yet!"

"Trying to set the mood, I guess," said the somewhat smaller-framed and clean-cut Joseph. "This is a ghost show, after all. Darkness fits the theme."

"Yeah . . . yeah, it does. And you know spirits don't like to show themselves in the open light."

"I don't think that's *really* why Professor Marvel has it so dark in here."

"Then why?"

1

"It's because if the lights were up, we'd be able to see the tilted glass on the stage, and the illusion wouldn't be as effective."

"Tilted glass?"

"That's right. What we're going to witness tonight, I suspect, is a variation of Professor John Henry Pepper's famous 'ghost machine.' A carefully controlled optical process that reportedly is quite effective."

"Professor Pepper? I thought the fellow putting on this show calls himself Professor Marvel."

"He does, but I suspect he's one of many imitators of the original ghost showman Professor Pepper, as he was called. He was a devotee of the sciences and a born showman. He developed, among other things, a means of projecting images, by use of a slanted glass and brilliant hydrogen light, that seemed to float in open air . . . very ghostly in appearance from the perspective of the audience. I think that is something like what we'll see tonight."

"So we won't see real ghosts tonight?"

"Do you believe in real ghosts, Liam?"

"I *think* I believe in them. I know I believe in *spirits*. Hang it all, if you do more than believe in God, you believe in a spirit world, right? Even if you think the only spirit is God himself."

"Logical thinking, Liam. But there's a big difference in believing in God and believing that some

2

traveling showman with the name Professor Marvel can actually summon up phantoms of the dead."

"Joseph, do you not remember our dear old Granny O'Keefe? She traveled all the way to Dublin to visit her old cousin, who had the 'power,' as she put it. And the pair of them talked to their own dead parents in the reflection of an old magic mirror. She told us all about it, remember?"

"Yes. And I remember it was hard to follow the story while she told it because she kept stopping to swig from that jug she could never do without. I think the spirits that Granny O'Keefe knew best lived inside that jug."

"You have a lack of faith, Joseph. And that surprises me, because you've always been by far the more religious of the two of us. You've given the priests a sight more confessions than I have, though I've committed a sight more sins. I'll have to commence my final confession at least six months before I die, just to finish up on time."

"I *do* have faith, Liam. But one of the things I have faith in is the supremacy of rationality. I recognize that most of the things we encounter in this world fall into patterns you can predict—cause and effect—and there is seldom reason to jump to supernatural explanations when natural ones will do."

Liam laughed aloud.

"You find that funny for some reason, brother?"

"Coming from you, yes! I can't believe I heard Joseph Carrigan, the king of supernatural explanations, say such a thing. You give a spookish, mystical explanation for everything you run across, Joe. You recollect when you were ten years old and you saw a cloud that looked like a dog, and at that time your new pup had gone missing, and you said that cloud was a sign from God that you were about to find your dog."

"And if you recall, we *did* find him, not five minutes later."

"Yes . . . lying in the middle of the road, dead as rock, neck broke by a wagon wheel."

"But we *found* him! That's the point."

"No, Joseph, the point is that the dang dog was *dead!* Hell, so dead he might just show up here tonight as a ghost."

Joseph wanted to argue but knew his brother was right. "Liam, I admit I'm prone to overexplain and overinterpret things sometimes, but for the most part, I'm a rational man—certainly more rational than you are, if you believe we're about to see something truly supernatural here. I know a fraud when I smell one, and if this performance is presented to us tonight as a true summoning of ghosts, as Professor Marvel's advertising would indicate it is, then a fraud is what we have. The people coming here tonight are hoping to see true shades from beyond the veil, not just a clever display of optical illusions."

The theater filled quickly. In this small town in the Montana Territory, Joseph had not expected to encounter such a level of interest in the Eastern urban phenomenon of the ghost show. Montana was known for level-headed, salt-of-the-earth, real-world types not usually receptive to swells and greasy showmen with contrived names like Professor Marvel. But Marvel had gotten the populace's attention. He'd stretched a big cloth sign from one side of Main Street to the other, announcing that he would be using his remarkable "mechanisms" to bridge the gap between the scientific and the supernatural and would invoke for those present the very spirit-images of dead people of prominence and even lost loved ones of those present in the audience.

It was Joseph who had insisted that he and Liam attend the show. Liam had argued against it. They had come to Montana seeking not ghosts but a living man: their own uncle, Patrick Carrigan, purportedly a rancher in this region. A ghost show was a waste of time in Liam's view.

Joseph believed it would be a waste of time, too, if the intent were actually to commune with the dead. But he had a sufficiently scientific mind to want to see just how effective Marvel's optical illusions could be.

Neither Carrigan brother had ever met the man

they'd come to Montana to find. Their uncle Patrick had come to America from their native Ireland years before Liam and Joseph's widower father had done the same, bringing his two young sons with him to raise as Americans. Their father, during what remained of his life, had tried sometimes to find his free-roaming brother but without success.

After their father's death, Joseph and Liam had gone on to several professional ventures with very little to show for any of them. A chance discovery of a newspaper clipping that lined a trunk someone had dumped off along a trail in Kansas led them to discover that their long-missing kinsman was still alive and apparently to be found in Montana, working the cattle business. Believing this discovery to be a sign that they were being divinely guided to seek their uncle, Joseph persuaded Liam that the two of them should begin a slow northwestern journey that, if successful, would end in a family reunion. Along the way to Montana, they'd already had a family reunion they had not anticipated, meeting a saloon fighter named, interestingly, Pat Carrigan. He'd proven to be their own cousin, son and namesake of the uncle they sought, though now estranged from him. The younger Patrick had given them the final pieces of information they needed to complete their quest, and now, here they were in the little town of Fire Creek, Montana, to do just that.

They were now near the place where Patrick Carrigan reportedly had his ranch and lands.

The feeble lamps that provided the only illumination in the theater suddenly dimmed. Liam looked around, studying the hard-to-delineate silhouettes of those around him, and marveled at the variety of human types who had come out on a Tuesday evening for something so bizarre as a stage show in which the dead were the billed performers. As his eyes slowly adjusted to the darkness, he saw several cattleman and cowboy types in the mix and noted that one particular cluster of these, seated on the opposite side of the theater, were quite intrigued by him and Joseph, staring at them as best anyone could stare in such a dimly lighted place.

Joseph noticed it, too, and commented on it to his brother.

"I see them," Liam replied. "I get the notion that they find us the most interesting thing here . . . and that doesn't make a lot of sense. We're just two strangers here."

"Maybe folks don't like strangers in these parts."

From some unidentifiable source, a light began to grow at the edge of the stage. Simultaneously, eerie violin music rose, so faint at first that Joseph was unsure he was really hearing it. One violin initially, then another, then two more . . . the musicians were apparently in a small orchestra pit at the base of the stage. The light continued to grow, then the curtain moved, and there was someone there, carrying a violin. Professor Marvel himself. He walked into the little circle of light and scanned the room, eyes not on the audience but above it, as if he saw things there that none other could. Joseph, rational as he sought to be about all this, couldn't suppress a cold feeling that crawled down the back of his neck like the brush of an icy hand. He had to hand it to Marvel for his ability to establish a morbid, frightening mood.

The showman raised the violin to his chin, then very slowly touched bow to string. He held that posture for half a minute or more while the unseen violinists made their music swell higher and louder, the harmonies ever more minor and dark. Then Professor Marvel drew the bow down as his fingers began a limber, amazingly fast dance high on the E string. The rapid music at first clashed with the underlying minor harmonies rising from the orchestra pit, but then began to mesh and bring unity to the musical disorder. Joseph felt his pulse quicken as Marvel's music transformed the atmosphere from dark dread to anxious expectation.

The music grew louder, speeding like the heartbeat of a man running from something horrifying. The rising light began to dance and quiver in time with the notes. Then the harmonies faded, and the violins played in unison, one then dropping out, and a second, a third, until finally Professor Marvel played alone. The melody grew stranger and slower, evolving back to the eerie tune that had started it all, this time played very slowly. And then, abruptly, Marvel threw the bow to the left side of the stage and the violin to the right. The instrument clattered and crashed to the stage floor, breaking its bridge.

"Dang misuse of a good fiddle, if you ask me," muttered Liam to his brother.

"The time has come!" intoned Marvel, his voice deep as a well and just as dark. "The spirits hover, eager to show themselves . . . spirits familiar, known to many of you here . . . spirits of the great and late, and of loved ones laid to rest in the soil but never laid to rest in our hearts. I warn you, ladies and gentlemen, what you will see tonight is no illusion, no trick of light and shadow, but the reality of spirits returning to the world of the living. Be not afraid, but do be respectful. The spirits are guests in our world of substance. Welcome them . . . do not offend them. For someday, all of us shall join their number!"

"Just as I thought, a fraud," Joseph whispered. "If he had any honesty about him, he'd say, 'Welcome, folks, to a performance that shows how skillfully scientific principles can be used to create a realistic illusion.'"

"Yeah, but this place would be about half empty if he said that."

"Bring on the spooks and boogers!" a cowboy with a strong Southern drawl yelled from the back.

"Be careful what you ask, sir, they are *here*. They hear you, and it may be that inviting their presence as you have will cause you to find yourself with a perpetual new companion, one who follows you long after our humble presentation tonight is ended . . . one who will lie beside you in your own grave one day, sharing forever your final space!"

"Pshaw! On with it, man! Hush the talk, bring out the spirits, and make 'em dance!" Another shout from the back, a different voice this time.

Professor Marvel suddenly struck a highly dramatic pose, hand up as if fending off something descending unseen from above. And the curtain opened slowly behind him.

Joseph strained his eyes, looking hard, and thought he did catch a barely visible glint of glass on the stage behind the showman. He'd never seen a performance such as this before, but he had read in magazines about how they typically worked, so what happened next was not unexpected. Even so, it was startling and far more believable in appearance than he had anticipated.

An image began to congeal above the Professor, a diaphanous, cloudy vision that seemed to float in the air and become more solid by the moment. Gasps and murmurs ran through the audience as the image became brighter and more distinct and took on a human aspect. Joseph felt Liam grow tense beside him, sitting up straighter, bearing down on his heels. Joseph glanced around at the rest of the crowd. The manifestation on the stage was now bright enough to cast a little light out over the assembly, so faces were more discernible than before. Everyone in the place was gazing raptly toward the stage goings-on . . . everyone except the largest man in the gaggle of cowboys who had earlier found the Carrigan brothers of such evident interest. He was a swarthy, big man with a thick shock of black hair and a seemingly dead left eye. He stared back openly at Joseph, a hateful expression on his ugly face.

Joseph forced his attention back to the show. Professor Marvel was ducking away from the manifestation above him, almost on his knees now, hands up as if to wave away the threatening spirit.

The manifestation now appeared nearly solid, though it retained some transparency. Through the white light that made up its incorporeal body, some of the trappings of the stage behind it remained visible. Joseph was surprised by how believable the illusion was. No wonder these shows had been sensations all across the country! To the uncritical eye, what was seen on the stage was a flesh-and-blood man being harassed by a transparent, weightless specter . . . a specter that wore a flowing, Indian-style robe and had the vicious look of the most cruel savage of some frontier child's nightmares.

"Back to the grave with you, Cornstalk!" Marvel shouted, suddenly lunging up at the ugly specter with something in his hand—a copy of the Bible. "In the name of all holiness, I command you to plague me no more, you wicked pagan!"

"Cornstalk!" someone exclaimed in the crowd. "That's Cornstalk himself up there!"

The expression on the face of the being changed, became darker, even more hate-twisted. The specter seemed to enlarge, causing a woman in the crowd to scream and bury her face. A man in the front row came to his feet and then fell to his knees, turning his back to the stage and unashamedly burying his face in the padded seat he'd just left, his arms over the back of his head.

The specter showed evidence of being able to see this, because it looked directly at the cringing man and reached for him. Its hand, with long, pointed nails, then extended toward the crowd. The occupants of the first two rows scooted back in their seats, and several other people in the theater hid their faces in their arms.

Marvel gave out a startling yell and lunged toward the spirit, waving the Bible like a weapon. The manifestation glared at him, seemed to reach for the Bible, and touched it. At the touch, it suddenly drew back as if burned, becoming smaller and looking now not so much hateful as frightened. The crowd noticed, and a few bolder members clapped and jeered at the cringing demon.

"Joseph, you ain't going to try to tell me that thing ain't real, are you?" Liam asked in a sharp whisper. "You couldn't make no illusion that good. That's old Cornstalk himself. The famous old Shawnee chief, sure as the world!"

"Oh, yes, it's real," Joseph said. "It's as real as you and me, and just as fleshly. That's the point. What you're seeing is no spirit, just an actor dressed in Indian garb and positioned in an area we cannot see from the audience. With lights played on him at carefully chosen angles."

"Then how can we see him up there floating around, if he's really standing offstage somewhere?"

"There's a huge tilted glass on the stage, Liam, giving us his image as a sort of reflection. Have you ever carried a candle toward a window at night? You see the candle, your hand, and as much of yourself as the candle illuminates, but you appear to be as deep behind that glass as you actually are in front of it. Your form seems to float in the darkness outside. The same principle is at work here. I can't tell you every detail of how it works, but I can assure you it isn't magic but science. And because this actor is practiced in his craft, he knows how to make his projected 'phantom' self reach out and touch things and move about realistically."

"Well, it's danged convincing to me. That looks like a real phantom moving around up there above the Professor. Say what you want, but if this is between science and magic, I cast my vote for magic."

"For God's sake, will you two be quiet?" a very large woman behind them scolded, rapping on Joseph's shoulders with the handle of a closed parasol.

Joseph winced. He'd not realized how loudly they'd been whispering. Even Professor Marvel was glaring at them from the stage.

"Sorry," Joseph said softly to the woman. He looked over his shoulder at her, and just as he did so, her eyes widened as she saw something obviously astonishing on the stage. At the same time, Liam almost came out of his seat beside Joseph.

Joseph whipped back around to take a look and was as startled as the others. The fearsome phantom of the old Shawnee chief was gone now, replaced by a new image, this one so familiar to all that he was instantly identifiable. It was the great Napoleon himself, in full uniform and in his most famous pose, hand thrust beneath one flap of his coat.

"Good God!" Liam exclaimed. "It's . . . it's that Frenchman . . ."

"Napoleon," Joseph said. "Or, more precisely, a short actor dressed as Napoleon, with his image projected optically in the glass behind Professor Marvel."

"You just know it all, don't you, Joseph? You just know everything . . . or you sure think you do."

"I certainly don't think I know everything, but I do know J. H. Pepper's ghost machine and the principles of applied optics that are behind it."

"The principles of applied optics," Liam repeated, imitating Joseph's slightly higher voice in a mocking, sarcastic way. "And who the deuce is J. H. Pepper? This fellow is named Professor Marvel."

"Pepper was the originator of this type of illusion. Marvel has refined his mechanisms, perhaps, but he is not the creator of them."

"Waterloo!" yelled Professor Marvel, evoking a shudder and a cringe from Napoleon. "Waterloo!" he called again and again, until the small-statured phantom had collapsed into an even smaller package and finally faded away in a flicker of dimming light.

George Washington appeared next, then Benjamin Franklin, Thomas Jefferson, and, at last, Abraham Lincoln. Lincoln's appearance brought jeers from audience members who had sided with the Confederacy, Liam included. But a reproving glance from Joseph, who had fought for the Union, quieted him, and Liam settled down for a long, bitter stare at the murdered president who had once represented all he and his fellow Confederates had struggled against.

"Joseph, that's him!" he said tensely. "Say what you want about glasses and light and opticals or whatever you call it, but that's damned old Abe himself! Look . . . you can tell it!"

"Liam, Abe Lincoln was shot to death. The image you see up there shows no sign of a wound that I can see."

"Who's to say that a man's shade will show every mark he suffered in life?" Liam asked. "Maybe some of that kind of thing doesn't show on a spirit body."

"Liam, ask yourself a question. Imagine that you're George Washington or Napoleon or Abe Lincoln. You've been dead for years. Does it seem likely to you that one day you'd just round up a few fellow ghosts of famous men and say, 'Hey boys, let's run over to Montana and manifest ourselves for a room full of small-town folks who've paid their five cents to see a ghost show'? Does that seem something that you would really do if you were so great a man as George Washington?"

"Not being a ghost myself, I wouldn't know."

"This is all optical trickery, Liam. Take my word for it."

"Take my word for it." Another mocking imitation of Joseph's voice.

Lincoln was still floating about above the stage,

looking out at the audience, his eyes dark and wise. Some of the same gaggle of cowboys who had been staring hard at the Carrigan brothers earlier seemed particularly offended by the presence of the fallen leader. One of them stood, drew a long knife from a sheath on his belt, and hurled it hard at the phantom. The knife flipped several times in its flight forward and hit the specter handle-first rather than blade-first. The ghost actually started, ducking down and throwing up a hand. At the same time, there was a loud cracking sound, like thick pond ice giving way beneath the weight of a heavy skater. Professor Marvel, who had almost been struck by the knife, let out a yell and gave a wild hand signal to some unseen assistant, and all at once, the phantom began to fade, light diminishing rapidly.

"The knife cracked the blasted glass!" Joseph said. "Did you hear it? It cracked it, and the Professor halted the display, so the audience wouldn't see it all come shattering down!"

"I didn't hear nothing shattering down. I just heard a snapping noise."

"The glass cracked but did not shatter," Joseph said. "But the Professor fears it will shatter, and he doesn't want the crowd watching when it does. So he's had his assistants kill the light."

Liam rolled his eyes and said, "Dear Lord Jesus, thank you for sending me a brother who knows as much as a human mind can know." He folded his hands at his chin in an imitation of prayer posture. "Thank you that, because of Joseph, I am spared going through life with the blight of ignorance upon me."

"Your sarcasm is offensive and unseemly," Joseph said. "Perhaps even sacrilegious."

"Hear that, Jesus?" Liam said to the ceiling. "I bet even *you* don't know as many three-dollar words as my brother!"

"Do not despair!" Marvel intoned to his audience. "The spirits have not flown! The manifestations will continue. Your loved ones linger at the portal, ready to show themselves to those among you who grieve their loss!"

"I want to see my Andy!" a massive woman wailed out from the middle of the crowd. "I want to see my poor lost soldier boy Andy!"

This pitiful plea made Joseph cringe and aroused in him anger at the showman on the stage. What gave any man the right to come to a town bearing hydrogen lights, optical lenses, and glass plates and, with no more than those and a flair for showmanship, create a vain expectation on the part of grieving people that they could actually reunite with loved ones who had passed out of human reach? Professor Marvel, whoever he really was, was a human vulture feeding on the sorrows and unrealistic hopes of his fellow man.

The room went almost utterly dark, and the crowd settled back, ready for a new wondrous display. But for a couple of minutes, only sound came from behind the stage, the sound of men working, moving things. Joseph leaned over to Liam. "They're taking down the glass, to be sure it isn't going to shatter to pieces because of that crack in it," he said. "And I doubt we'll see any more ghosts floating above the stage."

CHAPTER TWO

By the time the lights began to rise a little once again and the form of Professor Marvel grew visible, the crowd was restless. The cowboy who had thrown the knife got a reprimand or two from some old women in the crowd, but several others spoke in his defense. Chatter died away as the lights rose.

Marvel stood beside a strange but simple device, a wooden box on table legs standing about waist high. It bore odd, Arabian-looking markings on its side and had a thick glass plate on its top. Joseph deduced from Professor Marvel's posture and movements that the box had an opening or door on the side hidden from the audience. Marvel seemed to be manipulating something inside the box.

As before, Joseph had a suspicion of what Marvel was up to here and what the box probably was, but he decided to say nothing to Liam to avoid annoying him.

Glass clinked against glass, the sound somewhat muffled. Joseph was now confident that he knew what was going on. Marvel was mixing chemicals of some sort inside the box, probably in a bowl, beaker, or mortar. At any moment, smoke would begin to rise. Joseph had read about this kind of illusion. It was simply a smaller-scale application of the same principles that had manifested the images above the stage, with the variation of using smoke as the medium in which the "spirits" appeared.

As expected, chemically induced smoke abruptly spilled out through exit holes drilled around the sides of the glass atop Marvel's elevated box. Marvel backed away as if surprised by this, watching the smoke column thicken into a sort of moving pillar above the box. He cleared his throat loudly, coughed a little because of the smoke, then stepped around to stand in front of the box and address the crowd.

"We now move on to a portion of this exhibition that will be of great personal significance to many of you here," said the showman. "We have so far this evening seen the shades of great and famous men—"

"Nothing great about Lincoln!" yelled one of the unrepentant Rebels.

"Bring up John Booth so I can shake his hand!" hollered a like-thinking companion of the first shouter.

Marvel, who had a Northern accent, looked offended by this but merely raised his hand for silence, then continued. "We now shall see the spirits not of those whose names have made the history books and the newspapers but of those who are nearest and dearest to many of you here."

"My Andy! Bring me my Andy!" the big woman in the audience wailed.

Professor Marvel went back behind the wooden box. His hands were hidden from view again, but he was obviously manipulating something on the box. A light rose slowly, shining from inside the box and up through the glass atop it, illuminating the column of twisting and dancing smoke so that it looked almost like a phantom itself. "Behold!" Marvel intoned. "See if you find among these faces some whom you have known in this very town!"

"What faces?" Liam asked.

"Just wait," Joseph replied. "Keep watching the smoke."

The light grew brighter in the column of smoke, and suddenly something vague became visible, too dim to make out at first but gradually becoming more delineated, revealing itself as the miniaturized image of a man. But before the features attained a clarity sufficiently sharp to allow recognition, the image faded away. Another rose to replace it, this time becoming sharp much more quickly. Joseph noticed something about these newer, smaller, smoke-borne images that differed from the earlier and bigger phantoms. Those earlier, large images had exhibited a limited degree of color, but these new ones were cast purely in grays and blacks.

The image in the smoke column was by now quite distinct: a short man, stocky and muscled, with a large hammer in his hand. The motion of the smoke column lent an impression of movement to the figure, but a careful look revealed to Joseph that the figure was actually motionless, its look and perspective never changing, the mouth locked in a frozen smile, the eyes not blinking the way those of the larger phantoms had blinked.

Several people in the crowd stood, and voices erupted, none of them saying exactly the same thing but all of them in agreement on one fact: the figure in the column of smoke was John the blacksmith. Evidently, this was a man who had been known to many in the audience.

"Who is he, you say? John?" Professor Marvel asked the crowd. Then he addressed the smoky phantom. "John, I greet you and welcome you. Your friends are here, welcoming you as well. Join me, friends of John! Together now, on three . . . one, two, three—"

"Welcome, John!" at least a score of voices said in unison.

The column of smoke danced and twisted just

then, as if in response to the voices, though Joseph hadn't missed the quick but nearly hidden wave of the hand that Marvel had performed, fanning the smoke into motion.

"How are you going to account for *that* manifestation, brother?" Liam asked. "Are you going to tell me now that there's an actor in a costume hidden inside that little box, and that smoke is really just something on a plate of glass?"

"No . . . but you are closer than you know to the truth," Joseph replied. "You are seeing the projection of a photographic portrait that's hidden inside the box."

"I don't believe that," Liam scoffed.

"Why? Is it easier to believe this confidence man has actually summoned spirits? Why does it have no color, Liam? The others had color because there were live actors generating the images. These don't. Why? Because they are photographs."

Professor Marvel drew nearer the column of smoke and spoke in low, inaudible tones to John. At the same time, Joseph noticed, he again made a manipulation behind or in the box with his hands.

`And then John was gone, the smoke column empty. Not for long, though. In moments, another figure began to materialize slowly: a young man in a Confederate uniform. Marvel looked at this phenomenon as if surprised, then leaned almost into the smoke itself, turning his ear to the phantom as if listening to its whisper.

"Is there in this place a Mrs. Loretta Abernathy?" he asked the crowd.

The woman who had spoken earlier about her lost soldier boy Andy stood so fast she actually leaped straight up an inch or two. When she came down again, the floor vibrated; she was quite a large woman.

"Andy!" she exclaimed in a loud, emotional voice. "Thank God above, it's my own Andy, come back to see his mother!"

She began trying to make her way out of her row of seats, but it was slow going because of her size. She was almost to the aisle when a man dressed similarly to Professor Marvel appeared from the back of the auditorium, grasping her meaty arm. "Please, ma'am, you cannot go up there," he said. "Professor Marvel does not allow such close proximity between visiting spirits and those they come to see."

"Why not?" she demanded, clearly offended. "I'm Andy's mother. I'm the one he's come to talk to! I want to be close to him, to touch him!" She pushed the man out of her way and continued into the aisle.

"It really *is* your Andy, Loretta," said another woman from elsewhere in the room. "I can see him clear as a bell from where I sit. He looks just the same as he does in that picture you got on your mantelpiece, Loretta! Just the same!"

"That's because the image of him there in that smoke probably *is* the very same picture that sits on his mother's mantelpiece!" Joseph whispered.

Liam replied, "Wait a minute. Why wouldn't a man's shade look the same as he did in real life, if he took on a spirit body? And if he wanted to be sure his mother recognized him, might he not strike a pose that was familiar to her?"

"Don't be so blasted gullible, Liam!"

"And you don't be so blasted arrogant! You know it all, don't you! You think you know more than God himself, Joe."

"No, there's at least one thing he knows that I definitely don't, and that's why he ever suffered such a fool as my brother to be thrust upon this world!"

"He did it because there's one greater fool he knew would need some protecting, that's why. He sent me to keep an eye on *you*, Joseph!"

Somehow, Professor Marvel and his assistant managed to keep the excited mother from climbing onto the stage. She went instead to a small area at the side of the orchestra pit, as near as one could get to the Professor's magical box without actually being on the stage with it. There she stood, staring at the image of her lost son in the dancing smoke, wiping tears that rolled down her broad face.

Marvel leaned almost into the smoke pillar and whispered at the image. Then he turned his ear toward it and seemed to listen. He circled around the smoking box and knelt before the weeping woman. Leaning, he whispered in her ear, while her unblinking son stared at her from within the column of smoke. Mrs. Abernathy wept harder, but when she turned to go back to her seat, her face was beaming. Clearly, whatever word had come to her from beyond the grave had given her news she was pleased to hear.

"Now I don't know whether to despise Marvel or grudgingly admire him," Joseph whispered to Liam. "On the one hand, he is a great deceiver preying upon the sentiment of bereaved people, and on the other, he has just made that woman quite happy, no doubt telling her of her son's message of joyful existence in heaven. And tonight she will sleep, I expect, with greater peace than she has known since her boy died."

"Then I do admire him, and not grudgingly," Liam responded. "And say what you will, Joseph, I don't believe he is a deceiver. Would a grieving mother not know whether or not she was really seeing the phantom of her own son? Would she not?"

"She might not, if she were faced with a perfect presentation of her son's appearance."

Marvel called another name, a man's. Two rows behind the Carrigan brothers, a burly fellow burst to his feet and let out a yelp, his voice higher than his large and manly form would lead one to expect. The man slapped both hands over his mouth, staring with eyes as big as coffee cup rims at Marvel and his magical column of spirit-revealing smoke.

This time, the figure within the column was a woman, very small and frail, her hair pulled back tight around the sides of her head and hidden beneath a large, engulfing bonnet.

"Cynthia!" the big man said, his voice quaking. "My dear Cynthia!"

Liam whispered into Joseph's ear, "No wonder she died . . . he probably crushed her to death, if you know what I mean."

"I had the same thought," Joseph said.

Again, a trip to the corner of the stage area on the part of the bereaved, again a conversation between Marvel and the specter. Marvel knelt and spoke privately to the big man just as he had to Mrs. Abernathy. And the man wept unashamedly. "Thank God she is all right," he said in a voice loud enough for most in the auditorium to hear. "Thank God she's in heaven!"

Marvel patted the man's meaty shoulder and sent him back to his seat. Then the process repeated, with new phantoms arising one by one in the smoke and new individuals making the journey down to confer with Professor Marvel and receive whatever news from beyond the spirit had conveyed.

Joseph watched it all with a good deal of interest initially, but eventually the repetitive quality of it all became dull. He sank lower in his chair, laid his hands across his stomach, and closed his eyes. His awareness of what was going on around him diminished, and random absurd thoughts began to ramble through his mind like drunken stragglers.

He turned in his seat, found a more comfortable position, and drifted into a deeper slumber. Suddenly, Liam's leather-skinned hand gripped Joseph's forearm hard enough to hurt. Joseph's eyes snapped open, and he almost launched out of his seat

"Joe, Joe . . . it's Pa up there! It's *Pa!*"

Joseph, perplexed, blinked the fog out of his eyes and looked at Marvel's ghost box. He was so shocked by what met his eyes that he jolted back in his chair as if someone had kicked his chest.

In the column of smoke stood, in miniature, the very image of his and Liam's late father. The same hair, eyes, mouth, whiskers, even the same stoop of the shoulders. Despite the distance between himself and the stage, the small stature of the flickering image, and the distortion caused by the moving smoke, Joseph fixed his gaze on the image's eyes and felt as if he were yanked backward over the years and once again feeling the eye of his long-dead father.

Intellectually, he knew the truth: that the images

seen in the smoke column were, like those that had floated earlier above Professor Marvel, mere projections.

Yet a mystery remained. How would Professor Marvel have obtained a picture of their father, who died years before and very many miles away? And why? He did not know the Carrigan brothers or that they would be in his audience.

Then a realization came. He grabbed Liam's arm and made him turn toward him. "Liam, that's not Pa up there," he said. "It can't be. He's holding a rifle that didn't exist during his lifetime. See? They weren't making Winchester 1873 rifles before Pa died."

Liam looked at the smoke again, squinting. "If not Pa, then who?"

Joseph had a notion of a likely answer, but before he could speak it to Liam, there was an explosion of activity across the room among the gaggle of cowboys the brothers had noticed earlier. The biggest of the bunch was heading for the stage, his face fearsome with anger and determination. His eye was on Professor Marvel, who backed away fast as the big man mounted the stage. This one would not be content to linger beside the orchestra pit.

"What the hell is *this?*" the intruder bellowed, waving his hand toward the ghost machine and the smoke column, the wind generated by that motion making the smoke dance and distort itself even more. "Why is he showing up in that smoke? He ain't no ghost!"

Marvel stumbled backward, almost falling. I . . . I don't know who he is," he said. "I vow to you, I don't know."

The big cowboy marched across the stage to the ghost machine and looked through the glass at the top of it. "Damn!" he declared loudly. "Damned if this ain't the damndest fraud I ever seen! It's a picture, that's all . . . a danged picture, shining up into the smoke!"

"Did you hear that, Liam?" the vindicated Joseph said.

"I heard."

The man fiddled about with the back of the box, with Marvel looking on in distress. The intruder knelt and thrust his hand inside the box, then came out with a handful of photographs. He waved them above his head and spoke loudly to the crowd.

"Ain't no ghosts here, just pictures!" he said. "Look here, ma'am, here's a picture of your soldier boy Andy. That was what you saw, not his phantom. That was why that charlatan over yonder wouldn't let you get near his box. He didn't want you to see the pictures in the box!"

The crowd emitted a collective rumble of anger, and Professor Marvel looked around for the nearest door. But there was none. The mother of the fallen Andy began to cry loudly.

"Joseph," Liam asked, "how did Marvel get a picture of our father?"

"He didn't," Joseph replied. "That's not our father in the picture. Can't be . . . the rifle proves that."

"But if it ain't him, then who? It looks just like Pa. I mean, *exactly* like him!"

Joseph started to give his speculation, but the cowboy who had taken over the show suddenly stepped to stage front and aimed a long finger in Joseph and Liam's direction. "You two!" he called. "What do you know about this?"

"You talking to us?" Liam replied.

"Hell, yes, I am!"

"We know not a thing about it, friend," Joseph called back. "We're just two strangers in town who stopped in to see a ghost show out of curiosity."

"I seen how you reacted when you seen that last figure in the smoke!" the man called. "You knew him!"

"He happens to look like somebody we knew at one time," Joseph replied.

"You're a damned liar, and we both know it. I know who you are and why you're in Fire Creek, and I'm damned if I'll stand for it!"

"You apparently know a lot more than we do, compadre," said Liam. "We came to this town to mind our own business, and I suggest you take up the same habit."

"Oh, I'll mind my business . . . and if your business is what I believe it is, me and my friends over here will be seeing to it that your business never gets done around these parts!"

"What the deuce are you talking about, friend?" Liam demanded.

"Liam, let's get out of here. This show is over," Joseph said. "I don't see anything worth staying for now."

Liam nodded, and he and Joseph headed for the aisle. They moved toward the doors with a strong sense that many eyes were on them.

On the stage, the cowboy who had taken over the place wheeled to face a quaking Professor Marvel. "Where did you get the pictures you made your ghosts from?" he demanded.

Marvel looked pale and scared but did not reply.

"I smell Picturebox Steadman's hand in this!" yelled one of the other cowboys, and a generalized murmur across the crowd indicated others agreed with the thought, whatever it meant.

At the exit door, Joshua grabbed Liam's arm. "Did you hear that?" he whispered.

"I don't know what it means."

"I think I do. I noticed a sign out on the street earlier—Steadman Photographic Studio."

"So Picturebox Steadman is a picture taker."

"I would suppose, the Picturebox name probably referring to his camera."

"So what does that matter to us?"

"Think about it, Liam. If a local photographer gave those ghosts to Professor Marvel, then that picture that looked like our father most likely was a local man."

"Who, for God's sake? He looked *just like Pa*, Joe!"

"Think a minute, Liam. Get your logic moving again. Why did we come to Fire Creek?"

"To find our uncle. Patrick Carrigan."

"Maybe we just found him . . . or his picture, anyway."

Liam's brows shot up. "So that's why he looked so much like Pa!"

"It would make sense of a thing or two. Uncle Patrick is a local man. So Steadman might easily have a picture of him."

Liam and Joseph left the theater and exited to the street, where the light seemed intensely bright and made them wince and blink. Liam pulled Joseph over into a shadowed alleyway, where the ocular suffering was less, and said, "Listen to me, Joseph, and answer my questions. Bear with me if you don't see right off what I'm trying to get at."

"Go ahead."

"What kind of show did we just see?"

"A deceptive summoning of spirit manifestations."

"A fake ghost show, in other words."

"That's right."

"Fake . . . but the people who were shown were supposed to be dead folks coming back."

"Right."

"Then if they included Uncle Patrick in that show, it must mean he's . . ."

"Dead."

"That's right. Otherwise, why would they present him as a ghost?"

Joseph looked away. He'd thought the same thing on his own already but had not wanted to say it outright. It would be too depressing to think they'd crossed the country and gone through all the ordeals they had, only to find, in the end, that the man they thought they'd been divinely destined to find was dead.

Having seen the image in the smoke only made the prospect worse. If that truly had been Patrick Carrigan's image, then meeting him would be as close as they ever could come to seeing their father again. Unless somebody came up with a ghost performance that wasn't fraudulent.

"Joseph, what was behind the way that big fellow who took to the stage talked at us so threatening?

Who does he think we are, and what does he think our business is?"

"I have no idea, Liam. I can't know that any more than you do."

"Whatever he thinks we're here to do, he sure don't want us to do it."

"Did you notice one thing he said, Joe? He told Professor Marvel that the image of Patrick Carrigan—if that's who it was—didn't belong up in that smoke, because he wasn't a ghost."

"In other words, still living."

"That's what it would mean to me."

"I hope he is alive. I want to find him. More than ever now."

The door opened, and out came the oversized mother of the late soldier Andy. She was wiping tears, her face blotched and wet. "I wish I'd never come!" she said to a somewhat smaller, shorter woman who came out just behind her. "I had no notion that we were being presented nothing but fakery. I so wish it really had been Andy appearing to me tonight. God above, I miss him so!"

The woman almost ran into Joseph, who stepped to the side, touched his hat, and said, "Good evening, ma'am."

She looked at him quite hatefully and muttered something beneath her breath. Joseph gaped at

what he heard and watched her walk off the porch
and onto the street.

"What'd she say, Joe?"

"'Murderers,'" he said. "'Hired murderers.'"

"Talking about you?"

"About *us*, I guess. She spoke in the plural. Why
would she say such a thing as that?"

"I'd like to know. I'd also like to know why we were
of such interest to them cowboys in there. You saw
how they stared at us, and how the big one who took
to the stage called us down and talked about stopping us from doing our 'business' here."

"Yeah . . . I have no idea what he meant."

"Could those cowboys be thinking, for some reason, that we're hired killers? Somebody in there
must have said something, after we left, to put the
notion in that fat woman's head."

"Why would anyone think that, though?"

"Don't know. All I know right now is that I ain't
yet had no supper, and I'm nigh starved."

"Same here, Liam. Yonder's a café. Let's go."

They trudged across the street. As they entered
the café, Liam glanced back and saw others beginning to spill out of the theater. The entire crowd appeared to be vacating the place. The show was over,
it appeared. He drew Joseph's attention to the people
swarming out the door.

"I wonder if Marvel had to refund their admission cost?" Joseph said. "He was exposed as a fraud before their eyes, after all."

"If they did refund it, we should go back and get ours."

"It was just five cents, Liam. Let it go."

"It's that kind of thinking that puts a man in the poorhouse."

"I've just had my fill of Professor Marvel and false spirit apparitions and all that. And I'm very hungry."

So was Liam, so the refund suddenly seemed unimportant. The brothers proceeded into the café, and found a table by a front window. Hanging coats and hats on the backs of the two extra chairs at the table, they ordered steaks and coffee and settled in for a long, much-needed meal.

CHAPTER THREE

Coffee notwithstanding, Joseph again found himself feeling drowsy, and as conversation faded into a pleasant silence, he leaned toward the window and propped his chin on one hand. Slowly, he began to fall into a shallow sleep, as he had in the theater.

Liam sipped his coffee and looked around the restaurant, then out the window at the street. It was beginning to grow dark. He felt a little sleepy himself but decided not to fall asleep as Joseph had. They would look two fine fools, sitting there sleeping at the table when their steaks arrived. He took a deep sip of coffee and shook his head quickly to break out of his drowsiness.

They'd traveled far and hard to reach this place. No wonder they were tired. Liam was looking forward to that fine hotel bed tonight. He and Joseph had rented rooms already and put away their meager goods.

Good hotel rooms and steaks at a real restaurant. And when the meal was over, they could go for beers at a local saloon. It had not been as good as this at the start of their journey. They'd been as poor as two church mice. Their fortunes had improved along the way, though, and now they had sufficient means to allow themselves a few luxuries.

It wouldn't last forever, though. He hoped they'd find their uncle not only safe and sound but situated and willing to provide some employment to two nephews he'd never even met.

Liam was staring into his coffee cup, deep in thought, when movement at the window made him look up.

Just on the other side of the window, a man was standing and staring with intense interest at Joseph, who was leaned almost against the glass. It was the same big, strapping, one-eyed cowboy who had taken over the stage and exposed Professor Marvel's trickery, the same cowboy who had made those inhospitable challenges to the Carrigan brothers and threatened to keep them from their business, whatever he perceived that to be.

The man glared at the snoozing Joseph, his lip twitching almost like a snarl. Liam reached over and pulled back the curtain a little to give himself a better look. The movement of the curtain caused the man to see Liam, whom he apparently hadn't noticed until then. He frowned and stepped back, being faced now not by a sleeping stranger but by one who glared right back at him and looked ready to come through the window to get him.

Fire Creek was a town with no regulations against carrying pistols within the town limits. The big cowboy had a Colt holstered around his waist, and he reached for it as he and Liam exchanged glares. Liam was startled to see this. Was this town normally so unwelcoming to newcomers? Or was there something in particular about himself and Joseph that had drawn ire?

Liam slid his foot over and kicked lightly at Joseph's ankles, waking him up. Joseph sat up, blinking, and shook his head quickly to clear it. Liam flicked his eyes and brought Joseph's attention to the man outside the window.

Joseph frowned. "Him again!" he said.

"He's been staring at you as if you were Satan himself come to Fire Creek," Liam said. "Something about us has stirred up some real interest in that fellow."

Joseph, not liking being stared at, frowned back at the man and pushed his face almost to the window.

"Careful, Joseph, he might be loco. He might draw out that pistol."

"Well, I've got mine, too."

Liam actually chuckled. "Lord, brother, we've changed places. You're talking reckless, and I'm

41

telling you to be careful! We've got our usual pattern turned backward."

"I don't like a stranger staring at me through the window. I got a mind to go out and ask him why he's doing it."

"He's turning away, Joseph. Best to let it go."

Joseph saw that Liam was right and began to wonder if he'd merely imagined that the man had been looking at him at all. Maybe he'd dreamed up this whole thing.

But no. Thinking back to the theater, he knew he hadn't. The big cowboy had called attention to him and Liam right in front of the entire crowd. But his words had been cryptic; it remained utterly unclear why he and Liam were of such interest to a stranger.

A woman's voice rose on the other side of the café, drawing Joseph's attention. It was the woman from the theater, the mother of Andy the soldier, whose image had appeared in Marvel's smoke column. She was standing beside a table at which a family dined, speaking in a too-loud voice.

"Mr. Steadman!" she said. "A word with you, please!"

"Did you hear that, Liam?" Joseph asked. "Steadman . . . that must be the photographer who provided pictures to Professor Marvel."

The man outside the window was gone now, so the Carrigan brothers' attention shifted to the woman. Fortunately, her booming voice made eaves-dropping easy, and Steadman also was a loud speaker.

"What is it, Mrs. Abernathy?" the man at the table said.

"I want you to answer me something, Mr. Stead-man. Why did you provide a picture of my poor Andy to that fraudulent showman!"

"Mrs. Abernathy . . . I'm not sure I know what you mean."

"Don't lie to me, Stanley Steadman! I can tell when you lie—your left eyelid twitches like you're trying to shake a fly off it!"

"That's true, Stanley," said a woman seated beside Steadman, presumably Mrs. Steadman.

"Mrs. Abernathy, are you speaking of Professor Marvel?"

"I am. A fraud, he is. He presented himself as able to commune with the spirits of the departed, using his magical apparatus, and he created an image of my poor Andy in a column of smoke, but it was merely an image of his photograph, the same image you yourself created before he went off so bravely to war."

"I did provide the image, dear Mrs. Abernathy, but I did so in the purest of good faith, believing he de-sired pictures of the local departed so as to be able to identify them, perhaps, when they appeared during his performance."

"So you believed he could actually bring the dead back to appear before those of us still living?"

"I did. I spent my childhood in a house in which walked the shade of a man who died before this nation became a free and sovereign entity. I have seen too much of the other side to believe it cannot at times find its way into the world that we so arrogantly believe makes up the whole of reality. I had every reason to trust what I was told by the Professor."

Mrs. Abernathy touched a finger to the corner of her left eye, wiping away a tear. "I, too, believed in him, sir, so I cannot fault you. I have known you far too long, Stanley Steadman, to believe that you in any manner willingly participated in a cruel fraud. Forgive me if my questioning has offended you."

"You could never offend me, Mrs. Abernathy. But please, satisfy my curiosity. How did this showman utilize the photographs I provided him?"

"He placed them inside an ingenious lighted box, one that also produced a heavy smoke from a chemical concoction, and used the light to project an image of the photograph into the smoke. This he presented as the very spirit of the lost one—a cruel jest. The most cruel . . . and then, crueler yet, he pretended to receive communication from the spirit and passed this on to the deceived bereaved ones."

"Most cruel indeed," Steadman agreed in his too-loud voice. By now, everyone in the café was listening to the conversation.

Mrs. Steadman ventured a question. "Were his communications from the dead words of comfort or of sorrow?"

"Of comfort," Mrs. Abernathy said. "He had, at least, that much of mercy in him. He had my Andy telling me of the heavenly choirs he heard every long day of eternity and the joys of conversation with Jesus Christ himself."

"Such a wicked man will certainly never have the pleasure of such conversation himself, except in the status of the judged wicked facing the divine Judge of all."

"Amen, Mr. Steadman. Amen, sir."

"Wickedness surrounds us, Mrs. Abernathy. Wickedness most unexpected and of infinite variety."

"Oh, do tell, sir! Even in the theater of the fraudulent Professor Marvel—who I now suspect is no professor at all—there were men who have come to this town with the most wicked intentions there could be: the murder for pay of an innocent man."

"What's she talking about?" Liam whispered to Joseph.

"Well . . . maybe us," he said. "Remember what she said when she encountered us outside the theater? 'Murderers . . . hired murderers.'"

"But we ain't hired murderers, Joseph."

"No, but maybe somebody has somehow gotten the notion that we are. Maybe that's the business that that big fellow was talking about from the stage, the business he said he not allow us to do. Maybe we've been mistaken for two other men."

"That's a big leap of speculation, brother."

"I know. I know."

Their whispered exchange had cost them the hearing of the ongoing conversation between Mrs. Abernathy and Steadman. They reconnected with the exchange just in time to gain some information of great relevance to the matter just discussed.

"I cannot imagine how anyone could be so bitter, so evil. Can you imagine taking another person's life for money? Especially a good person like Patrick Carrigan."

"Joe, did you hear that?" Liam said in a tense, sharp whisper.

"I did."

"We need to talk to that woman."

She looked around just then, a general scan of the room, and when she saw the Carrigan brothers, her gaze locked on them, and her lips parted slowly. "Them!" she said, just loudly enough to hear. "There they stand! *Them!*"

Steadman twisted his head and saw the brothers, who quickly tried to act as if they were minding their own business, even though virtually everyone else in the place was also listening to the Abernathy-Steadman conversation.

"You're right, Liam," Joseph said. "Let's go talk to her. We need to know why we're getting all these odd reactions in this town."

"Then let's do it." Liam stepped forward and strode resolutely toward Mrs. Abernathy.

She immediately blanched, staggered backward a step, then turned and headed out the door as if someone had set her dress afire.

"Ma'am, please wait!" Joseph called. He was about three paces behind his brother.

Mrs. Abernathy did not miss a step. She was out the door without a glance back before Joseph could draw a breath to speak again.

Liam halted, then proceeded to the spot where Mrs. Abernathy had stood. He looked down at the Steadmans.

"Is your name Steadman?" he asked.

"You're a forthright fellow, Mister . . . Mister . . ."

"Carrigan. Liam Carrigan."

Steadman reacted strongly to the mention of the name Carrigan. He began to rise but lost his balance and fell awkwardly against his chair, almost tipping it. Liam raised his hands as if in mock surrender and said, "Relax, sir. No reason to rise up against me! I'm not looking for trouble, just information."

"Your name really is Carrigan? Or is that

just an inappropriate joke, like the picture in the smoke?"

"You've lost me, sir. I have no notion of what you mean. I've not made any jokes that I'm aware of since I came to this strange little town."

Steadman stood slowly and looked closely at Liam. "By George!" he said softly. "I can see the resemblance. You *are* a Carrigan!"

"I am indeed, sir. All my life. In fact, my father was brother to Patrick Carrigan, and it's him we've come to see."

Joseph, now standing near his brother, nodded.

Steadman tugged at his collar, ill at ease. "Gentlemen, may we step outside and talk?"

Both Joseph and Liam thought about the man who'd watched them through the window. Still out there, probably, and maybe looking for trouble. So going outside might be imprudent. But neither brother was the kind to hide, and they certainly couldn't huddle inside this café forever.

"We'll step outside with you, but you should know there may be a man out there looking for us, someone who seems to find us very interesting and we suspect has a false notion of who we are and why we're here."

"Oh . . . then let's step into the back instead. There's a small dining room that is usually reserved for meetings of the town council or the cattlemen's association, but it's empty now, and we can talk in there."

"I hate to take you away from your table," Liam said.

"Think nothing of it, sir."

The room was small, paneled with unfinished pine boards, and decorated with an old Indian blanket hung on one wall and the skull of a longhorn, complete with the horns, on the other. Joseph sat down, but Liam and Steadman remained standing.

"Mr. Steadman, sir, there's something I want to ask you," Joseph said. "There were photographs used in the supposed ghost show put on by the man who billed himself as Professor Marvel. Did you provide those photographs to Professor Marvel?"

Steadman stared at his boot tips a moment, looking ashamed. "Yes," he said softly. "But I did not know they would actually be used in the show. I was told by this showman that he needed them merely to be able to recognize the faces of the phantoms he would invoke with his fabulous machinery."

"I take it you have been creating portraits in this town for many years, then. Long enough to have portraits of many locals who have passed away over the years."

"As long as there has been a Fire Creek, I have been here," Steadman said. "There is hardly a family residing in or near this town whose images I have not preserved. Including many individuals who have since died, which is why this Professor Marvel came to me. He knew I could provide him with the images he needed—images that would be instantly recognized by those who would be in his audience here."

"But you had no suspicion he would use those images in a fraudulent manner?"

"No. You see, I believe in the possibility that we may actually be able to contact those who have gone beyond the veil. Thus, I believed him when he told me he needed the images merely for identification purposes."

"I see," Joseph said.

"Don't get red-faced over it," said Liam. "Joseph here is gullible, too."

"Liam, shut up," said Joseph. Then to Steadman: "There was one picture, one ghost that came up in the smoke of Marvel's machine, that apparently was the image of Patrick Carrigan. And that raises a question: Why did Marvel include Patrick's image before a crowd of people who would know he is not dead?"

Steadman scratched his chin, his eyes shifting from side to side. "I . . . I don't know I can give you any insight into that," he said.

"Can't or won't?" Liam challenged.

"It's all the same."

"Not hardly, my friend."

"Ease up, Liam," Joseph said. "Mr. Steadman,

just tell us this: Is Patrick Carrigan in fact still alive and well?"

"He's alive but, if the rumors are true, in grave danger."

"How so?"

"He has enemies . . . one enemy, really. And it is his plan, all talk has it, that Patrick Carrigan shall indeed be dead soon."

"When his image appeared in the smoke, there was a great reaction from several men seated on the other side of the theater. One of them protested that the image had appeared and declared that he was no ghost. And shortly after, he took to the stage and brought the show to an end."

Steadman said, "Might I seek to describe the man I believe this could be, and you tell me if my description matches that of the man who ended the show?"

"Speak, sir," Joseph said.

Steadman cleared his throat and gave a detailed description that did in fact match the man who had mounted the stage—the same man who had only minutes before stared at Joseph through the window of this very café.

"Who is this man?" Liam asked. "And what is his fascination with us?"

"And his association with Patrick Carrigan?" added Joseph.

"His name is Riley, Keefer Riley. He works for Patrick Carrigan—his ranch foreman, I believe."

"Wait . . . you're telling me, then, that this man is a friend and associate of our uncle?"

"Yes, that would certainly follow from what I just told you, would it not?"

"Well, yes, but what puzzles me is that the man exudes hostility . . . and why would that be? We are no potential source of harm for Patrick Carrigan. We're his own flesh and blood!"

Liam sighed. "Joseph, think for a minute! We know that what you just said is true, but this Riley doesn't."

"But why assume we are dangerous?"

Steadman cleared his throat. "I can clarify that for you."

"Speak on, then," said Joseph.

"I mentioned to you that your uncle has an enemy. His name is Bret Ellison, and, like Patrick Carrigan, he is a rancher. But a rancher of a much greater public stature and level of wealth and influence. He holds some deep grudge against Patrick Carrigan, and God only knows what it is. All I know, all anyone else knows, to my knowledge, is that Ellison holds the most hostile of attitudes toward Patrick Carrigan . . . so hostile that the two are considered to be literally at war with each other. Because of those two, and the factions that support each, there is an ongoing hostility in this region. There is war at Fire Creek."

"War . . . as in a range war?"

"Of sorts, though apparently not over the usual issues that spark such conflicts. There seems to be something very personal in whatever has them at odds, and it seems to be driven mostly from Ellison's side."

"What does this have to do with our uncle's picture showing up in a ghost show?"

"I don't know. All I can tell you is that I was visited by a representative of Professor Marvel and paid to provide all the images I could of local individuals who have died in the last ten or fifteen years and who still had relatives remaining alive here. And then I was specifically asked to provide an image of Patrick Carrigan as well. No explanation why. But I did as I was asked."

"I can only think of one significance to showing the image of a living person in such a performance. It was a symbolic threat, an implication that Patrick Carrigan is as good as dead. But why would a visiting showman have reason to even be aware of our uncle, much less threaten him?"

"I can't say, sir, but I smell the stench of Bret Ellison in this."

"Can you direct us to our uncle's ranch, Mr. Steadman?"

Steadman blanched and looked at Joseph with quite a strange expression. "I . . . I don't know that I should do such a thing, not really knowing you."

"We've told you who we are."

"Yes, but the fact remains that I have only your word, and you are two strangers asking after Patrick Carrigan. There is a significance to that at this place and time."

"What is that?"

"Rumors are rife that Bret Ellison has hired gunmen to assassinate Patrick Carrigan, specifically two associates, perhaps brothers or cousins, known to kill for pay. "

Liam and Joseph looked at each other in surprise. "That explains a few things," Liam said. "Like the reaction we got from that Keefer Riley fellow."

"Yes," Joseph said. "He works for our uncle, is protective of him, and no doubt knows that rumor and is on the lookout for strangers because of it. And here we show up, obviously brothers, and attend a ghost show where the image of Patrick Carrigan appears without explanation. And we reacted to it when it happened, and he saw that."

"He might also have thought we were the ones who arranged to have that picture put in the show to begin with," Liam said. "He might have figured we were making a boastful threat by putting that picture up there among Marvel's gallery of the dead, that we were sending a message that Patrick Carrigan would soon be as dead as the other people whose faces appeared in that smoke."

"Now we know why Mrs. Abernathy was muttering about hired murderers, too," said Liam.

"And I hope you can forgive me if I, too, have a lingering doubt about your intent," said Steadman.

"But you've already noted our family resemblance to Uncle Patrick," Liam said. "Is that not enough to persuade you we're being truthful with you?"

"You do resemble him, certainly, both of you do, but it could be coincidental. I could not live with myself if I unwittingly took part in guiding killers to an innocent victim. Not only innocent but positively good. I hold Patrick Carrigan in the highest of regard and cannot take a chance of doing him harm."

"I cannot fault your motives, then, but I find myself frustrated because I know who I am, and who my brother is, and that we are here to find Patrick Carrigan for the best reasons, certainly not to bring him harm."

Steadman's Adam's apple bobbed up and down. "I believe you, sir. Truly I do. But belief and knowledge are not the same. I cannot guide you to him until I know that you are who and what you say you are."

"I will not ask you to betray your own conscience, Mr. Steadman. I'm sure that it will not prove overly difficult to find our uncle's ranch. Such things are hardly secret."

"No . . . but among those who admire Patrick Carrigan, you may find the same hesitation you find on my part. And you could find yourself trouble, because the rumors of two hired killers coming for Patrick Carrigan are prevalent, and you may easily be misidentified."

"We'll be cautious," Liam said. "And if we happen to run into those hired killers ourselves, they'll find us more than a match."

"Liam talks big," Joseph said. "But he's right. We'll fight hard to protect our uncle . . . even though we don't yet know him."

"Good for you both, then. And I'm sorry that my foolishness in providing that picture of Mr. Carrigan to the showman caused problems for you. That being said, of course, on the assumption that you are being truthful with me regarding who you are."

"We are indeed, sir. I hope that we will have the opportunity later to prove that to you."

"Protect your uncle, men. He deserves it."

"We'll tell him you said that," Liam said. "When we find him."

"When you do find him, be cautious. He has probably heard the rumors, too, and he may not know you."

The brothers nodded. Neither of them had thought of that.

CHAPTER FOUR

No one lingered at the café window when Joseph and Liam left. Keefer Riley had moved on. The Carrigan brothers were able to walk to their hotel without any unpleasant encounters.

They'd rented rooms there earlier in the day. Adjacent but separate rooms, joined by a single interior door. They'd resided in several hotels during their journey across America—and several woodsheds, empty barns, abandoned houses, and once even a cave—and the Fire Creek Arms was one of the tidiest and most inviting lodgings they'd run across. And like Marvel's ghost show, it was an unexpected find. One did not anticipate encountering an excellent, new, three-story hotel in a little place like Fire Creek.

"So what now, Joe?" Liam asked as they entered their rooms and opened the door between them.

"For me, a little relaxation," Joseph said. "We're

not going to find Uncle Patrick tonight. And there's still some evening hours remaining."

Liam grinned. "Glad to hear you say that, Joe. I'm in the mood for a little relaxation myself. And I know just the place to start."

"So do I . . . that rocking chair over there, with my feet propped up on that stool and a good book off these shelves open on my lap. Look at that, Liam, a virtual library in each room! I'm impressed by this place."

"You and I have different notions of relaxation, Joseph. You talk about rocking chairs, and I'm thinking of that big watering hole we passed coming into town today. Remember?"

"Liam, you think it's a good idea to go out drinking in this town, considering the kind of reactions we've evoked here? Everybody from cowboys to old women is identifying us as hired killers come to town to do the worst. You get out in a saloon, and there's no telling what trouble you may find, or be found by."

"Always the worrier, ain't you? I can take care of myself, Joseph. If you want to spend a perfectly fine evening hiding up in a hotel room like an old granny with a book on your lap, then do it. But I'm going out to find a *man's* pleasures."

"Any chance you have in mind bringing one of those pleasures back up to your room tonight? Is that why you insisted we have separate rooms?"

"That, and the fact that you snore as loud as a train."

"Liam, don't go out consorting with whores tonight. I worry about what will happen to you. I watched a young fellow die back during the war from a pestilence he picked up from a whore. His legs and arms withered away into knobby, gnarled-up sticks, and he had huge, ugly, warty bumps all over his face and body. It was a death no man should have to endure."

Liam had no ready reply. He, too, sometimes worried about such things, for he'd also witnessed the ravages of venereal diseases during his military years. He'd been lucky himself, managing to avoid infected females, but a man could not expect the dice to roll in his favor all the time.

He knew that there was more to Joseph's concern than worry for his physical health. Joseph, ever the devout Catholic, worried about Liam's immortal soul. And sometimes Liam did, too, especially those times he allowed Joseph to persuade him to go to mass and felt the convicting sting of the priest's words.

He'd straighten out someday. He'd promised it to Joseph, to himself, and to the memory of his mother many times. Someday . . . but not tonight.

"Joseph, if I should happen to find a female friend tonight, I'll try to make sure she is healthy and pure.

And you never know, I may not even look for a woman. I'm more in a humor for a few drinks and maybe a couple of hands of poker. Don't worry about the poker. I'll keep myself under control. I'll not throw away our money."

"No, you won't—not my share of it, anyway. I've got mine tucked away safe and sound where you'll not find it. You want to gamble, you do it with your own cash, and don't come whining to me when you're broke."

"Joseph, I congratulate you. No doubt Mother looks down from heaven and feels great pride at having raised at least one of her sons to be a worrisome, fretting old maid. She couldn't have done better herself."

"I'm grateful she can't see the life you lead, Liam. She'd not be much proud to know how many of your days you've spent in saloons and gambling dens and dance halls. It would sadden her."

Liam, a man with a heart more tender than he usually liked to show, blinked rapidly and turned his face away. Joseph swallowed and felt a burst of guilt. It was wrong to use Liam's emotional attachment to their late mother as a stick with which to beat him.

"I'll behave myself, Joseph. I will."

"I know." He paused. "You're a good man, Liam. Your ways and my ways are not the same, but who's to say they should be? I have all trust in you, brother."

"Thank you, Joe. And I will behave myself."

"Listen . . . look out for trouble. Even if you don't look for it yourself, it might come looking for you. Keep in mind the rumors about hired gunmen."

"Two hired gunmen, not one, and tonight I'll be out alone."

"But you'll still be a stranger in town, and a lot of people saw us together at that ghost show. Just be careful, that's all I'm asking."

"I will be. You, too."

"What can happen to me, sitting in a chair and reading a book? I'll be fine."

"So will I. So long, Joe. See you later. Don't wait up for me."

"I won't. I'm about given out. I'll be sleeping in that rocker before I'm through ten pages, I expect."

With his feet removed from his boots and his toes free to wiggle, Joseph felt like a man sprung from a prison. He grabbed a book at random—an old copy of *Gulliver's Travels*—and plopped down in the rocker. After scooting a footstool into place, he placed his heels on it and let sore muscles and aching arches relax.

The lamp at his side burned a little too brightly and was tending to flicker and gutter, so he cranked it down a bit, opened the book, and began to read.

He'd read *Gulliver's Travels* years before, in boyhood, but remembered only bits and pieces of the story. Tired as he was, he found reading to be slow going at first. What kept him at it was a recollection of something he'd once heard: *Gulliver* had been a favorite book of a man Joseph admired, the frontiersman Daniel Boone.

Weariness, though, was stronger than will, and before long, the story Joseph read began to merge with vague and directionless dreams. None of it made sense, yet in his dream state, it all seemed to possess a coherence of sorts, even if he couldn't identify it.

He jolted awake when something thumped against his foot. He'd dropped the book. Picking it up, he shifted a little in the rocking chair, sank back further into it, and fell asleep again. His dreams came back, Gulliver and his tiny captors no longer a part of them. He began to snore quietly while romping across a mental landscape with the same ill-fated dog Liam had talked about earlier. In his dream, he was a boy of eleven again, far away from Montana and back in Tennessee, the taste of just-picked July blackberries fresh on his lips, the sting of briar scratches on his fingers, his beloved dog romping ahead of him through the thickets and grass, birds whipping through aerial acrobatics above their heads, dark flashing streaks against billowed white clouds.

A beautiful, wonderful, exhilarating dream . . . the years rolled back, the sorrow of friends and family lost to the grave erasing itself as the clock spun backward, the weight of adulthood giving way to the lightness of childhood. Joseph knew it was all but a dream even as he dreamed it, but it did not matter. This mental escapade was the very essence of goodness, of the best days he had known and would return to again at any moment if that magical opportunity were offered him.

Then the dream changed, the blue sky growing dark, the white clouds turning gray and then black, lightning dancing between them and then firing to the ground like a bolt hurled by an angry pagan deity. In his dream, Joseph felt cold, moist wind whip his face, and then he was in a different place from before, on a stony ledge on a bluff pocked by dark holes and caverns. As a storm built above and around him, rain began to drive down like hard, stinging pellets, making him wince.

And then he heard the screams. High, feminine, slightly muffled . . . Joseph shuddered. These were the screams of a young woman in great suffering and fear, and instinctively he wanted to do two contradictory things: find her and help her, and run away so he would not have to hear the screams again.

He stirred in his chair, knowing somewhere deep

in his unconscious mind that this was not merely a dream but a memory. The girl had been named Agatha; her surname had faded from memory over the years. The daughter of a sharecropper, she had been a feisty and loud child, especially around Liam, whom she'd clearly admired in a girlishly romantic way. Liam, older than she by several years, had never noticed, not that Joseph could tell.

In his dream, Joseph looked around and recognized the pockmarked bluff upon which he roamed, a cliff that stood near the Carrigan farmstead outside Nashville, the boyhood home of the Carrigan brothers. He heard the muffled screams again and was drawn to the cavern from which they came, just as he had been as a boy when what was now a dream was a present reality.

Joseph moved in his chair again, trying to will himself awake, because he did not want to find what he knew he would find inside that cave. But he did not awaken, the screams continued, and the dream continued, too. He saw himself advancing, as a child, into the cave, losing the daylight as he progressed, until at last he had to light his way by lighting up a candle stub he had carried in his pocket.

He followed her voice, stepping carefully in the little circle of light cast by his flickering candle. The screams grew louder, and he turned a bend in the passage and saw her, leg twisted and trapped beneath fallen rock, her body crushed uncomfortably against rough stone, and, worst of all, snakes around her— not dangerous ones, simple common blacksnakes such as those Joseph saw frequently in the Tennessee hills, but snakes nonetheless. The nightmare quality of them made him recoil.

But Joseph, in his dream, did not run, just as he had not run when he was a boy and this had been a real event and not just a dream. He advanced to the terrified girl, ignoring most of the snakes and snatching away those he could not ignore, flinging them deep into the darkness and then stamping about noisily to keep them from returning. He reached her, knelt, and found her tense with pain. Her hand clawed up and gripped his forearm, squeezing tightly enough to hurt. By candlelight, he studied the rocks that trapped her and determined how best to move them.

That night, when he fell asleep, he did so with the praise of neighbors, the local sheriff, and, best of all, his own father echoing in his mind: "You're a hero, Joseph. You saved that poor girl's life, you did."

He slept that night in great peace, until the dreams came. Dreams of snakes, crawling on him and around him, coming out of the darkness.

Something thumped against his foot, and he sat up straight in the rocking chair, blinking into the empty, lamplit room. For a moment, he couldn't remember where he was, and then it came back. And just then, he heard a scream, sightly muffled just like the screams in his dream. But no dream this time.

Another scream, a little louder and in a tone of greater desperation. Joseph stood and saw that he'd dropped the book on his toe. He turned toward the window, recognizing that the scream had come from outside, and as he did so, his hand knocked over the lamp beside his chair.

He caught it just before it would have rolled off onto the floor and somehow managed to grip only the cool parts of it and avoid a painful burn. The flame, though, went out, casting the room into darkness.

Joseph set the lamp back in place and went to the window, which was already partially opened. He raised it further and cautiously thrust out his head, glad now that the room was dark, for he could see movement in the alley below. If he was fortunate, they would not see him, with no light to silhouette him.

At first, he could not see well enough to make out anything specific, but soon his eyes adjusted, and he saw something that shocked him more than finding that girl in the snake-infested cavern back in his boyhood.

A man was lunging at a woman in the alley below him, but they were only partially visible, because a small overhanging roof that covered an alleyway side door to the hotel intervened between Joseph and the pair below. It was the woman's screams he had heard and which had prompted him literally to dream up a cause for them.

She screamed again; he heard it much more loudly now that his head was thrust out the window. He saw movement, bodies in motion but hard to make out in detail. He had an impression of the woman trying to run but being snagged by her attacker and pulled back beneath the little overhanging, canopy-shaped roof above that side entrance. Joseph felt helpless, too cut off from what was happening to be of any help.

Then she screamed again, and he knew he had to help somehow. Then came thudding sounds, like fists against flesh, and she cried out yet again.

The man was beating her! Joseph felt such a surge of rage that his common sense was overwhelmed. He ran back into his room, put on his gunbelt, and strapped the pistol firmly in place in its holster, then opened the window as far as it would go and put one leg out.

Could he do it? He was on the second floor, and the little roof over the door was not very far below. He should be fine if he could leap onto it, assuming it was strong enough to bear his weight and assuming he could keep his balance on its curving surface.

He heard more beating, more cries, and then

moaning, and he knew he had to do it, risky or not. What would Liam think of him, doing something so heroic and daring? Even as he prepared to launch himself out and down, he knew the answer: Liam would be proud and, in fact, would already have made such a move himself, if he were there.

Joseph balanced for a moment in the window, wondering if the pair below were aware of him, then said a quick prayer and leaped. The drop felt farther than it looked as if it should, but his leap was accurate, and he landed squarely on top of the overhang.

But the overhang was not strong and apparently was partly rotten, because Joseph's right foot went through the wood as if it were no more than paper. He went down all the way to the thigh and felt his boot heel strike strongly against something both hard and yielding. A masculine yell of pain came out from beneath the overhang, and he realized that by sheer luck, or perhaps divine aid, had just come down atop the head of the man below. A moment later, as Joseph tried to pull his leg back up through the hole again, he saw the man's form tumble out into the alley, facedown, hands groping at the top of his head.

Joseph managed to free his leg from the hole it had made in the roof but then teetered leftward on the sloping little roof and sensed, just before he fell, that he could not right himself in time. As best he could, he tried to make like a cat and land on his feet, but he only partially succeeded, coming down first on his left foot and turning the ankle, causing him to collapse.

The man he had booted in the head was moving, trying to get up. Joseph rose more quickly, though he could barely stand because of the pain in his ankle. He staggered to the side, turning, and for the first time saw the woman he'd leaped to rescue.

He'd expected someone helpless and cringing, but that was not what he saw. The woman appeared to be in her mid-twenties at the oldest, her hair blond and her build rather slight. Surely she would take advantage of the moment to run . . . but again he was surprised. Instead, she leaped directly onto the man who had attacked her, landing on the small of his back and literally running up his spine. Joseph heard the *oof* noise the man made as she drove the wind from his lungs. Just below the base of his neck, she actually leaped up and came down hard between his shoulder blades, to make sure all the air was knocked out of him. Joseph winced, wondering if she had broken the man's back.

The young woman wasn't worried about it. She gave her foe another jump between the shoulder blades for good measure, then kicked him stoutly in the head after she'd stepped off him. He groaned and rolled over, tried to get up, and she kicked him in the head again. This time he lay still.

The woman looked at Joseph in a way that froze him where he stood. Nothing wilting or afraid here . . . he wondered how the man who attacked her had managed to get even one scream out of such a seemingly fearless and ferocious creature.

She stepped a little closer to Joseph and looked hard at him, then knelt quickly and came up again. She now had the pistol of the fallen man in her hand.

"I've seen you before," she said. "Where's the other one?"

"I don't know you, ma'am."

"I saw you at the ghost show. You're one of the two folks were saying are the hired murderers everybody's been looking for."

"Not me, ma'am. Not me. My brother and I are just two traveling folk come to town looking for some kin."

She raised the pistol. "If you're lying, and if you so much as even try to lay a finger on Mr. Carrigan, I'll hunt you down myself . . . and I can do it. Don't think I can't."

"After what I've seen tonight, ma'am, I believe you could probably whip an army. But my brother and I have no intent to harm Patrick Carrigan. He's our uncle we've never known, and we've come in hopes of getting to know him and maybe work with him some."

"Uncle?"

"Yes, ma'am. Swear to God."

The moon had come out a bit, lighting the alley just a little. The young woman motioned for Joseph to step forward, then stopped him when he was situated in a shaft of moonlight. She looked at his face in concentration.

"You bear a resemblance to him . . . a strong one. Maybe you're telling me true."

"I am indeed. My father was Patrick Carrigan's brother. They grew up together in Ireland, and Father followed Patrick to the United States when Liam and I were just little boys. Liam is my brother. My name is Joseph. Joseph Carrigan."

"He has enemies, you know, Patrick Carrigan does. Especially Bret Ellison, damn him! Pardon my language, mister."

"I've heard about Ellison. He's the one they say has hired killers."

"Yes. And that's done nothing good for the way most think of that scoundrel. A lot of folks here admire Patrick Carrigan. They know him to be a good man. And they know that Ellison isn't. But people are cowards, afraid of Ellison and his money and the kind of men he surrounds himself with."

"How well do you know Patrick Carrigan?"

"Fairly well, sir. Fairly well. His son, the younger Patrick, I knew even better. There was a time he pined to marry me."

Now they were making some progress. Joseph knew the younger Patrick, having encountered him on the way to Montana.

The man on the ground moaned and moved again. Joseph looked at him, then at the young woman. "Ma'am, I'm thinking we should get hold of the local law. I don't know what intentions that man had in accosting you as he did, but I doubt they were good ones. He needs to visit the local marshal, or sheriff, or whatever you've got around here by way of law."

She shook her head. "It would do no good, sir. Not with the law here being under the thumb of Bret Ellison."

"Pardon me, but even if that is the case, why would that prevent the law from dealing with a man who mistreated a citizen in an alleyway?"

"Because of who I am, sir. Because in the mind of the local law, I'm part and parcel with Patrick Carrigan . . . I'm on the wrong side of the war."

War—the second time Joseph had heard that word used to describe the ongoing troubles between Patrick Carrigan and his enemy. A strong word, implying violence and danger. Just how bad was the situation at Fire Creek?

"Ma'am, would it be too forward of me to ask if you could tell me your name, given that you know mine?"

"I can't say I know yours . . . all I know is what you claim your name to be. You say you're Patrick Carrigan's nephew, and your looks back up that pretty strongly, but I don't really know that you're who you say. You could be one of those killers who just happens to be a right good liar."

Joseph was beginning to grow frustrated with this town. Nobody here was ready to accept a man's word for even the most simple facts, such as his own name. Again, he wondered just how volatile a situation he and Liam had drifted into.

Inspiration! He smiled at her, then said, "Ma'am, you tell me that you were close to Pat Carrigan, that he was ready to marry you. Did I hear you right on that?"

"You did."

"Then I'm willing to bet you knew his handwriting, correct? Probably got notes and letters and such from him?"

"I did."

"Well, I've got a letter in my hotel room up there, one Pat Carrigan wrote to his father, one he asked me to deliver to him. He scrawled on the envelope, too. I could show you that and prove to you that I really have been in the company of Pat Carrigan. That would go some distance toward verifying that I'm telling you the truth, would it not?"

She looked at him skeptically. "So you wish me to accompany you to your lodgings? Is that what you're asking of me?"

"Miss, please don't misread my intentions. All I ask is that you allow me to fetch that letter out of my room and show it to you. You can judge the handwriting for yourself. I would not ask you to enter my room with me alone. It wouldn't be fitting, and after all, I am still a stranger to you. But one, I should point out, who took some risk to help you just now. I jumped clear out of that window up there, and if I hadn't, you might be in a fix even yet."

She actually smiled at him, encouraging him. "You did make quite a heroic leap, sir. It was worthy of the stage, no question of that. But I don't know what your intentions were. Perhaps you saw a robbery in progress and thought to turn another man's work into your own."

"What? You mean, knock that man there out of action and take over in his place to rob you? Is that what he was doing? Trying to rob you?"

She brushed her right hand across the knuckles of her left one, a seemingly random nervous gesture. "It was. He sought to take a certain possession from me, the only thing of value that I own."

Joseph's eye was drawn to her hands because of

the motion she'd made. He squinted hard and made out a glitter on the ring finger of her left hand. "That ring?" he asked. "He was after your ring, maybe?"

She drew her hand back against herself protectively. "Yes," she said. "He wanted the ring that Pat gave me."

"Pat Carrigan?"

"Yes . . . the younger Pat."

"Is that an engagement ring?"

"Sir, you ask me too personal a question."

"I do, and I apologize for it and withdraw that question. Forgive me." He hoped it was not an engagement ring, because he knew that even at this moment, Pat Carrigan the younger was in Colorado with another young woman, April McCree . . . or perhaps by now she was April Carrigan. But if the ring this woman wore was a ring of engagement, the fact that she continued to wear it seemed an indication that she still believed herself bound to marry the man who gave it to her.

"You need not apologize. It was a natural question, and I am perhaps too prone to protect my privacy. And I shall answer you. It was indeed an engagement ring at the time Pat gave it to me, but the engagement did not last. I tried to return the ring to him, but he would not take it. He insisted I keep it as a remembrance of our friendship, if no more than that. And I have. It is a beautiful ring, and quite costly. I treasure it."

"I'm glad this scoundrel on the ground didn't succeed in stealing it from you."

"Yes." She looked down at the ring. "That engagement was a costly one to the Carrigan family. Not just in the cost of this ring but in the relation between Patrick the father and Pat the son."

"Ah . . . so the elder Patrick did not favor the engagement?"

"On the contrary, he was strongly in favor of it. It infuriated him when Pat developed doubts about whether the marriage should happen. They argued and grew apart from each other."

"I knew from the time I spent with Pat that he and his father were estranged. I did not know why, and he would not say."

"He's as private in nature as I am."

"Apparently so." He smiled at her. "You are determined not to let me know your name, I think."

"I am Charlotte Canaday."

"It is my honor to know you, Miss Canaday."

"Thank you, sir. And it is my honor to know you as well . . . if you are who you say, and if you indeed have not come here to harm or kill Patrick Carrigan."

"I would not want to harm a man I have crossed a nation to find, as years before my own father crossed an ocean to find him. Come, I'll fetch that letter and let you see the hand it is written in. You will know then, at least, that I have been in the presence of a man you were once betrothed to marry. That should lend me some credibility in your mind, I hope."

CHAPTER FIVE

The man on the ground moved again and groaned loudly. Joseph seized Charlotte's arm. "Miss Canaday, if we are not to turn this devil over to the law, let's at least get out of his presence. Else we may find ourselves in a row with him again."

She nodded. Joseph led her to the side door beneath the porch roof onto which he'd leaped and found it unlocked. It led into a hallway, lined with shelves on which stood empty buckets, crates of goods, and stacked bed linens and towels. A storage area, clearly, but as they followed it, it led them to a small door that opened into a more public hallway on the hotel's lowest floor. No one was about, for which both were secretly happy, because both were cognizant of appearances and what would be the natural presumption of those who saw a man and a woman sneaking out of a hidden area in a hotel.

Joseph did not worry for his own reputation, for he

had none in this town apart from the suspicion that he was a hired killer, but he did not want to contribute to any false notions regarding Charlotte Canaday.

They climbed the staircase and again encountered no other people. Joseph led her to his door, then took the key from his vest pocket. "Will you come in with me?" he asked.

"I can't. I might be seen."

"I understand. I'll fetch the letter quickly."

"What does the letter concern?"

"It is a private communication between Pat and his father. I have not read it and cannot show anything to you beyond the envelope that holds it."

"Very well."

Joseph entered the room and left the door ajar a couple of inches, mostly so he could keep half an eye on Charlotte. He lit a lamp, removed the letter from a drawer, smoothed some crumples on the envelope, and went back to the hall.

"Here it is. Pat Carrigan wrote his father's name. Do you recognize the hand?"

She moved into the shaft of light coming from the open door and looked closely at the envelope. Joseph watched her expression soften. She looked up at him. "This is Pat's writing. I would know it anywhere I saw it."

"Then will you help me get that letter to Pat's father, my uncle?"

"I'll take it to him, if you wish."

"My brother and I have come a long way to find him. We have nearly been killed more than once along the way. I'd prefer that we be able to hand that letter to him ourselves."

She frowned. "I'm sorry . . . I can't help you. Because you have a letter written by Pat doesn't prove you are who you say you are or that your intentions are good ones."

"Then I don't know what else I can do to prove to you who I am."

"Let me take the letter to Patrick. I'll tell him about you and leave it to him whether he wants to meet you or not."

Joseph wasn't completely satisfied, but her offer presented the most sensible solution to the standoff. Clearly, nobody in this town was going to lead two strangers to Patrick Carrigan voluntarily, not with the hired killer rumors so strong.

"Do it, then," Joseph said. "But promise me you will not read that letter. Liam and I made a firm vow that it would go only to Patrick Carrigan. I would not have that vow compromised."

"You have my word," she said.

"That's good enough, then. Take the letter. Guard it, and give it to my uncle. And tell him where Liam and I are and that we want to meet him."

"I'll do that."

She turned and walked down the hall, and then she was gone.

Joseph returned to his room and looked out the window through which he'd exited earlier.

The alley was empty. The man who had attacked Charlotte was gone. Joseph closed the window and wondered who the man had been and why Charlotte had been so reluctant to involve the local law in her problem. Could it really have been for some reason besides her claim that the law was under the control of Patrick Carrigan's nemesis, Bret Ellison?

And might the attack against Charlotte have been something other than an attempt to steal a diamond ring? For that matter, was her name really Charlotte at all?

She had been unwilling to take Joseph at his word regarding his identity and intentions, but he'd accepted everything she'd said at face value. Now he wondered if he'd been gullible. Maybe she didn't even know Patrick Carrigan.

And he'd just given her that letter.

He looked at himself in the mirror. "That's something like Liam would have done," he said to his reflection. "Sometimes you're not a smart man, Joseph."

It was just then he heard the scream, and right after it a gunshot.

* * *

Liam drained the shotglass and plopped it down loudly on the table before him. Wiping his lips with the back of his hand, he looked across at his drinking companion, a deeply bronzed and leathery man with a thick shock of white hair and the rumpled clothing of a cowboy or rancher who didn't change his garments any more than absolutely necessary. A further confirmation of this was given by the unwashed and earthy smell his person exuded. The smell had been offending Liam's nose ever since the fellow sat down.

But the man, who had introduced himself as Skillet Simmons, had two qualities that led Liam to overlook his smell and accept his company. One was his open and friendly manner, the other the fact that he insisted upon buying Liam drink after drink. Liam hadn't paid for even one of the whiskeys he'd consumed since he'd entered the saloon.

"Ready for another round?" Skillet asked after Liam slammed down his glass.

"Nope. That's all for me. Any more, and I'll not be able to stagger back to my room."

"Why, bosh!" Skillet said. "One more never hurts. In fact, one more always makes a man feel better."

"A man's got to know his limits," Liam replied. "I passed mine two drinks back. Why you so determined to get me drunk, anyway?"

"You remind me of somebody I think the world of," Skillet replied.

"Who's that?"

"Patrick Carrigan. You know him?"

"Never met him in my life. But I knew his brother. That was my father."

Skillet's gray eyes widened, and he slapped his hands down on the table so hard that Liam's empty shotglass rattled and fell over. Liam caught it as it rolled off the table.

"I should have knowed it!" Skillet declared. "I can look at you and see the look of him so plain. I'd have placed you as Patrick's son if I hadn't already knowed his son and that he had no others! So you're his nephew!"

"I am indeed. Me and my brother both. His name is Joseph."

"Well, then, welcome to Fire Creek, Mr. Carrigan. You and your brother both."

"Thank you! Glad to be here . . . I think."

"Why wouldn't you be?"

"Because you're the first human soul we've met here who didn't believe us to be hired gunmen come in to kill Patrick Carrigan. It seems a notion nobody can shake off."

"Ah, them rumors. I've heard 'em, too. So has Patrick."

"You know him pretty well, I take it?"

At that moment, there was a muffled pop of a gunshot fired somewhere else in town. It was not loud enough to be startling, but Liam recognized it for what it was.

"I been the cook at his spread for six years. He's like a brother to me. I know him better than most do. Well enough that there's no mistaking that family look I see in your face."

"So you're a cook. I wondered how a man got a name like Skillet."

"In my case, son, it was give to me by my very own pappy. He was a cook himself, back in Ohio. He named me after himself. And I become a cook because there ain't much else a man can do with a name like Skillet."

"I see your point."

"Where's your brother?"

"Back at the hotel. Reading a book, I think."

"Hell, that's no way for a man to spend an evening! Not with saloons open around the clock."

Liam liked this man. Liked the way he thought, the way he drank, the way he talked. And he liked the fact that Skillet actually trusted and believed him when he said who he was. "My brother can be a bit of an old woman sometimes," Liam said. "Come on, let's take a bottle over, and I'll introduce you to him. Maybe you can make him loosen up his collar a little."

"I'll do what I can, Mr. Carrigan."

"And maybe you can introduce Joseph and me to our uncle sometime soon."

"We'll do it tomorrow, sir. I'll be glad to do it."

"Thank you, Mr. Skillet."

"Just plain Skillet. No Mister."

"All right. And I'm just plain Liam."

"I'll pay for what remains in our bottle here. Then we'll take it with us and see if we can't persuade your brother to imbibe a bit of it with us."

"Sounds like an excellent idea to me, Skillet."

Liam walked at Skillet's side through Fire Creek, thinking about that muffled gunshot he'd heard and wondering what it might mean. Probably nothing. But he worried about his brother. If Joseph had left his room and gone out roaming, he might have run into trouble in this hostile town.

Odd that it should be so hostile here, Liam reflected. It was an appealing place to see, the very kind of little town he could imagine himself settling in someday. If only the local populace could get past this delusion that he and Liam were killers for hire.

Skillet gave Liam a town tour as they progressed toward the Fire Creek Arms. He pointed out this business and that, identified the houses of various residents whose names, of course, meant nothing to Liam, and labeled the churches by denomination. He paused outside a dress shop and talked at length about the "fine and beautiful Agnes Dorchester" who operated it and how he'd come within "pissing distance" of marrying her once. But it had all fallen through when she fell in love with a man who later became mayor and wed her on the big covered porch of the town hall. Being married to the mayor had made her "uppity," Skillet said, and now he didn't regret having missed out on his chance at married life.

They rounded a corner and came within view of the Fire Creek Arms, just in time to see something that jerked Liam to a halt.

Joseph, hands cuffed behind his back, was being roughly led out of the hotel by a man with a badge on his shirt. Joseph looked distressed and nervous, and the deputy had a pistol jammed into his side as if Joseph were a terrible desperado bound to make a break for it at first chance.

A gaggle of other people followed the deputy and Joseph. One was a young woman, quite pretty, who instantly caught Liam's attention, another a man in armbands who looked like a hotel clerk, and a third a tall fellow with a bloodied bandage on his arm. At sight of this man, Skillet reached over and grabbed Liam's forearm.

"That man there with the bloodied arm . . . that's George Clifford, and he's pure trouble. As sorry as they come, really. For the most part, a paltry thief who robs folks of their purses and valuables in back alleys and so on. But on the worser side, he's also an Ellison man. Does dirty work for him, and Ellison ain't above having dirty work done against them who fall out of favor with him. I have cause to believe that George Clifford is the man who took two prize collie dogs from your uncle's ranch, hauled them out, and killed them, then had them skint and their hides made into a coat that Ellison wears to this day. Ellison denies the pelts came from them two missing dogs, but everybody knows. Everybody knows."

"Good Lord!" Liam said. "This war between Patrick Carrigan and Bret Ellison sounds like a petty squabble between two boys, instead of a manly dispute."

"Ellison is like that . . . petty. I guess that's why he ends up associating such as Clifford there with himself. But Ellison is also dangerous, and there's not a soul at Fire Creek who don't know that his ultimate intent is to see Patrick Carrigan dead and buried."

"What sparked his hatred for my uncle?"

"There's the thing, young man, nobody knows. Or, at least, nobody's telling. Even Patrick don't know what it is. Or won't say."

"How long the two known each other?"

"For many a year. They've got history going back earlier than either of them coming to Montana. And there, I believe, is where you'll find the roots of the Fire Creek war. Hey, Liam, is that fellow in the cuffs—"

"Yes. That's my brother. That's Joseph."

"He must have been the one to shoot Clifford, then. Too bad he only hit him in the arm."

"I'll find out what's going on."

The little entourage had made it by now across the street and nearly to an intersection with the road that led to the local jail. Liam angled across and cut them off so as to be able to talk to Joseph and the deputy guiding him along.

The deputy reacted strongly to the sight of Liam, removing the muzzle of his pistol from Joseph's side and aiming it at Liam's chest. "Halt there!" he called to the approaching man.

"Whoa, deputy, hold on now. I'm not looking for trouble. It's just that you've got my brother all trussed up there, and I want to know what's going on."

"Brother, you say?" The deputy looked at Liam's face, then Joseph's, and gave a curt nod. "Well, you look enough alike that I can believe it. But you back off, brother, for I've got to take this one on to the jail. He's shot a man. Mr. Clifford back yonder."

"Just let it be, Liam," Joseph said. "Let him take me on. I'll get this settled."

"Why'd you shoot a man, Joe?" Liam asked.

"I'll talk to you later. Things aren't exactly what they appear to be."

The deputy gave Joseph a nudge, and the group brushed past Liam and continued on to the jail. But the young woman in the group broke off and stepped right before Liam, looking into his face. "You have to be his brother," she said. "Liam, he said you were named. I like that name. It's pretty."

"Thank you, miss. You're pretty yourself."

She glanced out to the street a second. "You're with Skillet."

"Yes, miss. I just met him a while ago. Seems a very good man."

"He is. He works for Mr. Carrigan, and he's good and loyal to him."

"So he's told me. Miss, can you tell me what has happened here? Why did my brother shoot another man?"

Her eyes filled with tears, and her lip trembled. "He didn't," she said. "He didn't shoot him. He just told them he was the one who did, so I wouldn't get in trouble. He's saved me again, twice now in one night."

"Saved you?"

"Yes . . . once from robbery and now from being arrested. He's taken the blame that should go to me."

"Wait . . . you're saying that you shot the man, and Joseph is taking the blame?"

"He did it himself. I didn't ask him to." She grabbed Liam's shoulders, surprising him, and made him face her squarely. She looked deeply into his eyes. "You erase all doubt," she said. "Looking at you, I can see there is no doubt you really are Patrick's nephews. You are the very image of him, even more than your brother."

"Miss, this is all very confusing. I don't even know who you are."

"My name is Charlotte Canaday. Your brother saved me from being robbed tonight, at great danger to himself. Then, when the robber returned again and I was forced to shoot him, Joseph heard the shot and came to where I was. He got there before the deputy came and took the blame for the shooting."

"Why?"

"I think because he is a good man. And he knows that I am close to his uncle Patrick . . . *your* uncle Patrick."

By now, Liam and Charlotte had been left behind by the others. "Miss Canaday, I need to go to where they are taking Joseph. I have to help him if I can. And after what he's done for you, I hope you'll help him, too. By telling the truth."

"You mean, telling them it was me who shot Clifford?"

"I don't think it would be right for you to let Joseph take the blame. And they'll not hold you at fault, not if you were defending yourself during a robbery."

Her face was glum. "You don't understand," she said. "The law here is under the thumb of Bret Ellison. They'll believe whatever they want to believe, and since I'm associated with Patrick Carrigan and Clifford is associated with Ellison, they'll take whatever view of this does me the most damage. It won't matter that I was being robbed. Clifford will deny it, and they'll take his word for it above mine."

"Skillet over there told me that Clifford has a history of street robbery. Surely they'll take that into account. They'll believe you."

"You haven't lived at Fire Creek. You don't know how things are around here."

"No. Maybe I don't."

Skillet, who had lingered in the street at some distance, came to them. "Hello, Miss Charlotte," he said, tipping his big hat.

"Hello, Skillet." She put her arm around his barrel-sized torso and gave him a hug.

Skillet winked at Liam. "As you can see, I'm much loved by the pretty young ladies."

"Oh, Skillet!" Charlotte said, smiling. "You never give me any peace from teasing me!"

Skillet hugged her back. "Liam, this is my girl here. Like a daughter to me. She's a fine one, and me and Patrick both know it. She was going to marry Little Pat at one time. But the fool let his eye wander and lost his chance."

"You're talking about Pat Carrigan? Patrick's son?"

"That's the one."

"I know him. I met him this very year."

"Yes," Charlotte said. "Joseph told me about it. And showed me the letter he wrote to his father."

"What letter?" asked Skillet.

"I'll tell you about it later on," Liam said. "Right now, can we go find my brother?"

Charlotte said, "If I need to confess, I'll confess. I'm the one who shot George Clifford, Skillet. Not Joseph Carrigan. Clifford was trying to rob me, take my ring away."

"Dear God . . . *you* shot him?"

"That's what I just said. But Joseph took the blame, to keep me out of trouble. But I'll not let that stand. I can't let him go to jail in my place. It isn't right."

Liam spoke. "Miss Canaday, I may be having a change of heart. Perhaps you should let things stand as they are for now. Maybe Joseph knows what he's doing. And if the law here is as corrupt and leaned toward Ellison's side as you say, you would have no chance of fair treatment."

"But neither will Joseph, once they learn he is Patrick's nephew."

Skillet said, "Charlotte, you may as well tell the truth. Because you know Clifford is going to, and they'll believe his version. He's not likely to go along with Joseph's version and let you get off the hook, not after you put a hole in him."

"I'll tell the truth," she said. "I've made up my mind. It's the only right thing to do."

* * *

The jail stood near the town hall but was not strictly a town operation. Fire Creek was one of those towns that relied on higher levels of government for its law enforcement, though it legitimized that dependence somewhat by paying the sheriff and his deputies a stipend to double as town marshal and police force.

Liam was provided little opportunity to speak to his brother, and when he did have his minute, he had to talk to him in the presence of a uniformed policeman. Joseph was seated at a small table in a room off the side of the office of the sheriff, and Liam was allowed to sit across from him for one minute, but only, he was told, because he was brother to the accused.

The atmosphere and general tone of conversation on the part of the law enforcement officials present seemed more suited to a multiple murder case than a mere wounding of a robber, it seemed to Liam. It made it easier to believe the allegations that the local law operated under the influence and to the benefit of Bret Ellison. He had a grim feeling that a great fist was being put in place to close around his brother.

"Joseph, listen to me. I talked to Charlotte Canaday, and she realizes she shouldn't let you take the blame for something she did. She said coming in here that she's going to confess the truth."

"I wish she wouldn't," Joseph said. "I don't trust the law here." He said those words in a whisper to keep the listening policeman from hearing. "I'm told the law here is run by Bret Ellison, a man I've already come to despise even though I've never met him."

"Same here. And I hear the same rumor . . . which is all the more reason for you to let her tell the truth. They'll show no mercy on someone with the last name of Carrigan, especially given that you're Patrick's own nephew."

"But they'll also show no mercy to Charlotte, for she's as good as a part of Uncle Patrick's family to them. And it isn't gentlemanly to let a woman suffer when a man can take it in her place."

"But it ain't just, Joseph. Hell, we don't really know yet how bad this war is. They could drag you out of this cell and hang you, for all we know."

"Now, there's a thought to brighten my spirits."

"We've got to look at things square in the face. There's a mighty odd situation in this place, and I think a dangerous one. Think about it, Joe. We came here, checked into a hotel and put our horses in the livery, and figured to have us a quiet night and celebrate finally being at the end of the journey. Then we go off to a ghost show, and all at once everything falls to pieces. And it all revolves around this war between our uncle and this other powerful rancher. And now you're locked up in a jail, accused of shooting a man you didn't even shoot."

"No, but I did do him some damage." Quietly, Joseph related the story of how he'd detected the robbery in progress and gone out the window to intervene, and how he'd driven his boot through the little roof to stomp the robber on the head.

Liam listened closely, intrigued and impressed by his brother's heroic actions. "I like to think I'd have been as brave, especially with such a pretty girl as that one being endangered."

"I thought of you as I did it—thought it seemed a thing more typical of what you would do than what I would do."

"I'll take that as a compliment."

"It's so intended."

"Joseph, what the devil is wrong with this place? How could one evening have turned into such a ruckus?"

"I don't know, Liam. Right now, I should be sound asleep back at that hotel, not a care to my name. And you, too."

"But here we are."

"Here we are."

The deputy stuck his head in the door. "Time for you to go," he said to Liam. "Got to talk to my prisoner, fill out some papers."

"Tell the truth, Joseph," Liam said as he got up.

"I'll do what you would do in this situation."

"No, don't do that. Tell them the truth."

Liam walked out, hoping the best for his brother.

* * *

The interrogation took an hour, and Liam heard much of it. Not Joseph's words, for he spoke too softly behind the closed door, but the deputy's shouts. Clearly, Joseph was frustrating him in some manner. Liam grinned. He could almost sympathize with that deputy.

At length, the interview ended, and the deputy opened the door and stormed out, barking something to one of the uniformed policemen. The policeman entered the room and led Joseph out.

"Did you get it straightened out, Joe?" Liam asked.

"I did what I should."

"You took the blame."

"Got to go, Liam. They're locking me up for the night."

Liam muttered a foul word and felt disgust at his brother, even though he understood perfectly what he was doing and would have done no differently himself. When Charlotte had shot that robber, she'd done just what she had the right to do. No gentleman would stand by and let a woman suffer legal consequences for doing no more than defending herself. Liam would have lied, too, would have taken the blame.

But in this strange, warring town, it was hard to predict what trouble might come to Joseph for his chivalry. His was not a safe situation, especially given his last name. Not in this town.

Liam walked out through the office and to the door. There Charlotte Canaday met him, looking deeply worried. "Did they let him go?"

"No. No, he told them he shot that robber, and they locked him up."

Her eyes filled again. "What a brave, good man to be so self-sacrificing!"

"That's my brother. He was raised to be a good man, and he is one."

"He's just like Patrick and Pat. Brave and courageous and looking out for other people."

"I guess he is. That's a good description of Joseph. But I worry what will come of this. Him being a Carrigan, they may make this hard on him."

"I know. That's why I have to go tell them the truth."

"But what will happen to you for doing that?"

"That I can't know. Maybe they'll be of a humor to let me go, given that I was defending myself."

Liam had his doubts but kept that to himself.

Another deputy approached just then, leading in a prisoner. The prisoner was a stoutly made, well-featured black man whose arms were so muscled they almost burst the fabric of the shirt he wore. The deputy kept farther back from this man than Joseph's captor had from him—clearly, he was afraid of him. But the black man was disarmed; the deputy carried his prisoner's gunbelt draped over his shoulder like the strap of a hunter's pouch.

Liam stepped aside and let the prisoner and the deputy enter. The deputy steered his prisoner back to the same room that Joseph had left.

A uniformed officer standing nearby shook his head. "Going to be a busy house here tonight," he said.

"How many cells you have?" Liam asked.

"Five. Plus another couple of rooms back in a separate building at the rear of this one. The original jail, it is, and it has a couple of cells that still can be used when things get crowded up in this one."

"Are you to capacity tonight?"

"Not yet, but if it keeps up like this, we might be."

"I want to ask you a favor," Liam said. "I want you to lock me up here tonight. Just like a prisoner. Not in that extra jail out back but in this one."

"Why you want that?"

"Because my brother is locked up here, and I want to keep an eye on him."

"Ain't nobody going to hurt him. We take good care of our prisoners."

"No doubt you do," Liam said, then proceeded to lie. "It ain't you I'm worried about. It's him. I'm afraid he might do harm to himself. He got locked up once before, in California, and he tried twice to hang himself with strips from the bedsheet. Good thing they didn't hold. He was a lot fatter at the time, and they couldn't bear his weight."

"Good Lord!" The deputy looked concerned, clearly believing every word of what Liam had just said, though in truth it was all a complete fabrication. He and Joseph had never set foot in California, and the devoutly Catholic Joseph would be the last man in creation ever to attempt to kill himself.

"Well, hell. I reckon it won't hurt to lock you up with him, if it would keep him from killing hisself. We don't need folks thinking we can't take care of our own prisoners."

"Thank you. I never thought I'd be thanking a man for agreeing to lock me up in jail, but I am."

Joseph had settled in fairly comfortably by the time Liam was brought to his cell. Liam looked around at the setup of the jail. The cells were placed on both sides of the building with a wide aisleway between them to allow the lawmen plenty of room to walk without worrying about being grabbed from between the bars. The cells on either side were in actuality built as one large cell divided into smaller ones by crosswalls made of masonry with large barred windows, so that prisoners could communicate between cells.

Joseph was lying on his back on his bunk, his hat

over his eyes and his hands laid on his chest like a dead man's, when the deputy rattled his lock and admitted Liam.

"Got you a cellmate, friend," he said. "This desperado look familiar?"

Joseph sat up and blinked in perplexity at his brother. "Liam? What have you done to get yourself locked up, too?"

"It was easy. I asked."

"Why?"

"You know that tendency you have to try to suicide yourself when you get into a jam, Joseph. I told them I was needed in here to keep you alive."

"That's a bigger pile than any I ever stepped in during our cattle-driving days, brother."

"Don't listen to him, deputy," Liam said. "I guarantee you he was lying there trying to figure out the easiest and surest way to end his sorry existence."

"That's nonsense!" Joseph protested.

The deputy wasn't interested in the debate. "You two behave yourselves. You won't get away with it if you don't."

Then he locked the door and left them alone. Joseph glared at Liam. "What's this bilge water about me trying to kill myself?"

"It did the job, didn't it? I'm not worried about you hurting yourself, Joseph. I'm worried about somebody else hurting you. Everybody I speak to tells me that the law is in this Ellison's back pocket. I don't know what might happen to a Carrigan locked up in Ellison's jail, if he hates Uncle Patrick as much as everybody says."

"So you decided that whatever bad fate that might be, it would be best if two of us suffered it instead of one. Is that your thinking?"

"I figure it's less likely to happen if there's two of us to resist it."

"What are you looking for? A lynch mob? There's nothing going to happen here tonight, brother, except for me and you sleeping on hard jail bunks instead of comfortable hotel beds."

"I just wanted to be here to keep an eye on things, and on you. Is there something wrong in that? You're my brother, Joe. I care about what happens to you."

Joseph smiled a little. "I truly appreciate hearing that, Liam. I do. And I'm glad to have you with me, truth be told."

"Good. How comfortable are these bunks?"

"Not very."

"Ah, well. I'm sure I've slept on worse."

CHAPTER SIX

Liam's bunk was on the side of the cell opposite Joseph's, located under the barred window that opened into the adjacent cell. Liam was nearly asleep on the hard bunk when the door of that neighboring cell opened with a terrible squeak, and a deputy's loud and grating voice cut through the murk of Liam's dozing.

"Here you are, boy your new home for tonight. Guess that'll teach you that Fire Creek ain't a town where we put up with negroes who get themselves into fights."

Liam sat up and looked through the bars into the next cell. A deputy he'd not seen before was shoving in a black man, of average height but heavily muscled and with fine, well-formed features. The floors of the cells were made of thick stone tiles, and one of these was unevenly placed in the newcomer's cell. His foot caught on an up-tilted edge, and he stumbled badly, falling in the direction of the window through which Liam watched.

He came almost face to face with Liam, who reflexively ducked back. The black man caught himself on the window bars and managed not to fall completely onto the bunk, then lowered himself and sat down on it. He continued to stare at Liam, looking at him in a way Liam thought odd and slightly unsettling.

"You all right, boy?" the deputy asked in a perfunctory tone. "You always that clumsy?"

"I'm fine," the man replied, still looking at Liam.

"Don't fall no more. I don't want to have to come in here and scrape black boy off the floor." The deputy winked at Liam as he said this, as if to say, *We white men know how these darky boys are, don't we?*

When the deputy was gone, Liam looked at his new neighbor. "Did you hurt yourself falling?"

"No. Stoved up my toe a little, maybe. Nothing that matters."

"Name's Liam."

"My name is Sparks, Mickey Sparks. I'm a cowboy."

"Good to meet you, Mickey. Me, I'm a cowboy, a shopkeeper, a bartender . . . anything I got to be to keep myself in food, shelter, and the occasional whiskey."

"I like my whiskey, too. Had some tonight . . . and that may be part of what got me in here."

"You don't seem drunk."

"I ain't. Just feeling a little warm in the belly, you know what I mean. My problem is I tend to fight a bit, and that's what got me in trouble tonight."

"Who'd you fight with?"

"Big tall fellow. Stranger in town. Looked like Abe Lincoln, believe it or not. Just like him."

"I do believe you. I saw the man myself, I suspect. He was part of a ghost show they had here in town earlier this evening. He played a ghost . . . Lincoln's ghost."

"No!"

"It's the truth."

"Was there real ghosts there?"

"No. Just actors. And pictures and such that got shone up onto a piece of glass, or some smoke, so that they looked like spirits floating around. But it was all a fraud. They even showed one fellow up there as a ghost who is still alive and well." Liam grinned, then noted the intense way Sparks stared at him. "Pardon me, but is there something about me that bothers you or interests you in particular? You look at me in a way that could drill two holes right through me."

"I'm sorry . . . don't mean to. You just make me think a lot of somebody else. A rancher hereabouts."

Over on his own bunk, Joseph turned his head to look toward Liam and Sparks when he heard that.

"Don't tell me: Patrick Carrigan," Liam said.

"Yes, sir. That's who you make me think of. Hell, you look the very spitting image of him to me. And so does that other fellow in there with you."

"That's my brother, Joseph. Joseph Carrigan. We're Patrick's nephews, though we've never in our lives had the chance to meet him. The family got broke up years ago, and we've come to Fire Creek to find him."

Sparks shifted to a more comfortable posture and leaned into the window. "You came here to find an uncle you never laid eyes on before?"

"That's right. We did. Came most all the way across the country. We didn't even know what he looks like until we saw him in the ghost show."

"Ghost show? He was there?"

"Not really. His image was, though. He was one of the ghosts."

"But Patrick Carrigan ain't dead. He has a ranch out southwest of Fire Creek. He's alive, unless something's happened I ain't heard about."

"You know him?"

"Not from lately. But we've met."

"I look forward to meeting him . . . I think."

"You ain't sure?"

Liam collected his thoughts. "Let me tell you how it's been. We showed up in this town, and from that moment on, all we've had happen is that we've run across people who are all worked up about Patrick Carrigan and another man hereabouts whose name is Bret Ellison. It appears the pair of them are at war one with the other, and there's a rumor about that Ellison has hired two killers to come in and get rid of Uncle Patrick for him. So here's me and Joseph showing up in town, two strangers, looking for Patrick, and folks get suspicious that we're the killers. Then they take a look at us and say we look just like Patrick, but nobody can be sure what to think of us. Nobody's willing to lead us to him just in case we are those hired killers."

"Are you?"

"Lord, no. We're his nephews, and we've got no ambitions at all to see him harmed. Quite the contrary."

"You an interesting man, Mr. Liam Carrigan. Tell me your story. I got time."

Liam was tired, but Sparks's interest motivated him. He paused, collected his thoughts again, and recounted in brief the entire saga of his and Joseph's search for their uncle—how it began with the finding of a newspaper clipping on the prairie, one that persuaded Joseph that they were literally being divinely guided to seek their uncle. He told briefly of their adventures along the way to Montana and the new leads and confirmations they had encountered, and finally he presented the story of the evening they had just experienced and how it led them to the unexpected destination of a small-town jail cell.

"It's strange when I consider it. This evening has followed a pattern. Everyone we encounter seems to say the same things to us, to half believe what we tell them and half doubt us and think us murderers for hire. I'm going to risk sounding like my mystical-minded brother Joseph here and say that the way things have happened tonight gives me the sense of something falling together as if by a plan, or destiny. Do you believe in that kind of thing, Mickey?"

Sparks let out a slow breath. "I do indeed, sir. The story you're telling me, it reminds me of things my old grandmother used to say about the world and the way things work in it."

"What do you mean?"

"She used to say that the world is made up of balances, all trying to keep themselves level. But sometimes a lot of those balances get knocked off the mark, and when that happens, things begin to happen to make them try to right themselves again. And that's what you're seeing when you see patterns starting to show theirselves. The balances are trying to get right again."

"How so in this case?"

"Well, maybe your uncle and your father never were really supposed to part from each other like they did. Maybe when they did—when your uncle left your home country and came to this one—maybe that threw off the balances, and things weren't right. So as the balances tried to right theirselves, your father got called to this country, too, called to find him, and when he didn't, then the task was just moved on down the line to you, his sons. Finding that newspaper clipping like you did, that wasn't no accident. That was evidence . . . evidence that the balances are at work. Things are trying to settle out and be put right again, and you fellows are just caught up in the flow of that, like leaves that have fell into a rushing stream, you know. That's what my old grandmother would have told you, anyway."

"Your grandmother must have been quite a philosopher."

"Oh, that she was, sir. That she was. A wise woman, a woman who could see things others couldn't. She could feel the balances of the world, feel them tilting and pulling and settling and all that. She talked about them all the time, and folks laughed at her. But not me. I believe in what she said."

Joseph sat up in his bunk and looked over at Sparks. "I think I believe in it, too. I think your grandmother and I would have seen a lot of things in common in how we believe the world works."

"I ain't so certain about such things," Liam said. "I'm prone to believe that most things just happen, kind of without reason, and it takes the minds of folks looking at them to make patterns start showing up. The minds impose the patterns on the world, instead of the other way around, if you know what I'm trying to say."

"With all respect, sir, I think you're wrong," Sparks said.

"That's fine, Mickey. I spend my life in company with a brother who constantly tells me I'm wrong . . . wrong about almost everything I open my mouth about."

Joseph asked, "Mickey, what about you? Are there balances moving and guiding you as well?"

"Yes indeed, sir. There's balances trying to right theirselves, and it's up to me to see that they do. It's up to me to cause it to happen."

"What's your story, then?" Liam asked. "You know ours. Can you share yours?"

Sparks sighed again and seemed quite uncomfortable. "I wish I could, sirs. I do. But there's reasons I can't. Not yet. But before it's done, maybe you'll see my balances getting settled out with your own eyes."

Liam and Joseph both wondered what he meant by that, but neither pursued the rather cryptic, esoteric matter. The night was growing later, weariness settling in hard and deep. The brothers lay back on their bunks and relaxed, Sparks quit talking, and the jail grew quiet until a deputy brought in two more prisoners and packed them into a cell on the other side of the jail. These were drunks, and drunks of the worst kind: singing drunks. The pair began a concert of barroom songs, and neither had a pleasant voice or any apparent ability even to approximate correct pitch.

Suffering under this most miserable lullaby, the Carrigan brothers at last went to sleep.

But Mickey Sparks did not. As the brothers snored, he rose and paced his cell, pausing often to look into the adjacent cell at the two sleeping brothers. He frowned and shook his head. "I'm sorry, sirs," he said in a whisper only he could hear. "I got my own balances to right, and mine and yours can't balance together. They just can't. Patrick Carrigan's got a debt he's going to have to pay, just like the others did."

He paced the cell until two in the morning, then at last lay down and slept.

Keefer Riley saw the light burning in Patrick Carrigan's window as he rode onto the grounds toward the ranch house. It was nearly midnight, and the morning would come early, but he wasn't surprised to see his employer still up and in his work room, as he called the chamber in his house that he used for an office. When Patrick Carrigan had things on his mind, he would sometimes pace away half the night or more, "working things through until they make sense," as he was prone to say.

Riley dealt with his horse and smoked half a cigar

before he trudged from the stable toward the ranch house. He could see Patrick through the window, pacing back and forth, hands in motion as if he were talking to someone, though Riley knew he was alone. "Tie up Patrick Carrigan's hands, and he couldn't think a thought," the old cook named Skillet often had said. Riley believed it.

Watching his boss pacing about inside, Riley pondered that Patrick should be more careful; a good marksman could drop him right inside his own house, shooting through the window. And in the current climate, a sharpshooting assassin wasn't an unrealistic fear.

Riley's boots clumped loudly on the porch as he approached the front door. It was no accident, just his way of letting Patrick know he was there. Patrick's head, covered with shaggy, graying hair that accented his drooping gray mustache, came near the window and looked out at Riley. He vanished at once and a couple of moments later was at the door, opening it.

"Well, Keefer, you're back at last. How are things in town tonight?"

"Very strange, Patrick. Worrisome and strange."

"You went to that ghost show, did you?"

"I did."

"What happened? Has it spooked you or something?"

"Not in the way you might expect. But there was a thing or two that happened there that leaves me puzzled and worried. About you, in fact."

"Ah. Don't tell me, you saw two strangers in town and figure Ellison's widely rumored hired killers have made their appearance."

"As a matter of fact, there are two strangers in town. But I don't know what to make of them."

"Why's that?"

"Because they both look so dang much like you, Patrick. They look more like you than your own son does . . . hell, they could *be* your own sons, from the look of them!"

"Coincidence, surely."

"Too close a resemblance to be coincidence. I got a close look at both of them, through the café window. I was as close to them as I am to you right now. They look like you would have looked some years ago. I'm telling you, Patrick, they're relations. Got to be."

"I'm not aware of having any relations in this country," Patrick said, his voice touched anew by an Irish brogue that had lightened considerably over the years. "I left behind my brother in Ireland; he might have married and had children, but I don't know that, and as far as I know, he never left the Isle."

"Don't take offense at this, Patrick, but have you ever had any dalliances with women you may not have been married to? Any chance of a few bush babies out there somewhere?"

"None. I was always faithful. Pure as the very saints."

"Well, good. That's a good thing."

"So there's two strangers in town who happen to look like me. And this at a time when there's supposed to be two strangers showing up to kill me and thereby brighten up the life of Mr. Bret Ellison."

"Patrick, one of these days you're going to have to tell me what the source of the trouble is between you and Ellison. I got a right to know. I could be caught in the crossfire when he finally gets you in his sights."

"He's not going to kill me."

"How do you know? He means to do it, I can tell you that."

"How so?"

"Because you showed up in that ghost show this evening. As a ghost."

"What?"

"It was all a fraud, I can tell you that. The ghosts were no more than images that got lanterned up into smoke or onto some kind of screen, but one of the images was you. A picture of you that the showman got from Steadman the picture man, or so I believe."

"Now, why would he put up an image of me as a ghost, since I'm as alive as anybody else?"

"I think that Ellison was behind it. I think he had

that showman do it as a way of telling everybody there that you were going to be a dead man soon."

"You really think that?"

"Why else would it have happened?"

"I don't know. I wasn't there."

"No . . . but those two strangers were. And you should have seen how they came to life after your image showed up. They reacted strong, Patrick. Strong."

"Well, if they look as much like me as you say, I can see why. Wouldn't you react if you saw the image of someone who looked like you being presented as a ghost? Probably they thought it was one of them being seen in the smoke."

"I don't think that was it."

"You think this is the pair who are supposedly coming to kill me?"

"I don't know. But I don't like them being here, not at a time like this. Not with all the rumors floating."

"You believe the rumors?"

"I believe Ellison is a wicked man, and yes, I believe you're in danger. I believe Ellison hates you enough to kill you. And I believe you know why he hates you, yet you won't tell me or anybody else. Why, Patrick? Why the secrecy?"

"Because some things are best left not talked about. But listen to me, Keefer. I want you to do something for me. Go back to town. Find those two strangers, and see what you can find out about them. I don't intend to spend my time dodging every strange face that appears in Fire Creek. Let's find out if they're worth being afraid of."

"I'll do all I can, Patrick."

"Fine. And in the meantime, I'm going out to the old line camp. I'll be safe there, hard to find, and it would do me good to get away from this place for a spell."

Riley shook his head. "Patrick, don't do that. You'd not be safe there at all. Ellison knows about the line camp. Everybody knows that's your escaping place. Why do you like that place so much, anyway? Nothing out there, just that lousy little hut. Most men I know would rather have a tooth pulled than be stuck in a line camp, yet you go there because you want to."

"I like it for the very reason you said: nothing out there. Nobody to bother you, nobody coming to call, nothing to be done except enjoy the wide, empty world. Everybody needs a place like that."

"Patrick, don't go there just now. If something happens to you out there, nobody would even know. If you stay here, we can keep an eye on you."

"I don't like being doted over, Keefer. I'm going to the line camp, and I'll be fine. And I'll come back in a day or two."

"You better. Because I'll be damned if I'm going

to let the likes of Bret Ellison kill the best boss I ever had."

"Kind of you to speak so, Keefer. Now, if you'll excuse me, I think I'll head to bed. I'm going to set out early for the camp."

"Wish you wouldn't go."

"I'm going. You come out and see me there, tell me what you find out about our two new visitors to Fire Creek."

"I will. As quick as I know anything, I'll be there."

Patrick looked out the window, and something caught his attention. He craned his neck, looking hard.

"What is it, Patrick?" asked Riley.

"Somebody's here, just came into the yard. Not much light, but I swear, I believe it might be Charlotte."

Riley looked. "Yeah, that's Charlotte. Well, I'm going, Patrick. You consider changing your plans about the old line camp, will you?"

"I'll consider it. But I'm set on going."

"You're stubborn. Danged stubborn. It'll get you killed someday."

"Probably will. Probably will. But a man ain't meant to live forever, huh?"

The sheriff was a burly man named Cordell Tyler. Confederate veteran of Shiloh, one-time criminal, and longtime purported enforcer of the law, he was a man who knew how to survive. And in Fire Creek and its environs, survival meant being sure to stay on the right side of one Bret Ellison, the most powerful figure in these parts.

Ellison was on Tyler's mind as he arrived in the early-morning light at his office. As sheriff, he allowed himself the luxury of letting deputies handle law enforcement duties during the night. He was a daytime man and worked nights only when required by circumstances.

He'd already talked to a deputy whom he'd encountered at the edge of town and had learned the intriguing fact that two strangers were in custody in his jail, one of them under arrest in a brawling incident, the other, apparently his brother, locked up because he asked to be.

Two strangers . . . could they be the men he was expecting to show up?

According to his deputy, this pair had an oddity about them: both bore a strong resemblance to Patrick Carrigan, of all people. Tyler was eager to see that for himself. How ironic it would be if Ellison's two hired killers wound up looking like the very man he wanted them to kill!

Hired killers . . . Tyler found the thought of such distasteful. He was far from a straight-arrow lawman, in fact was corrupt and knew he was corrupt, sold out to Bret Ellison for a monthly "bonus" that came to him in a brown envelope delivered by one of Ellison's house maids. Usually, Ellison sent Allie, the pretty one, and Tyler liked that. He had a feeling he could get more out of Allie than that envelope, if he ever tried. Maybe next time he would. He was a widower, after all, no wife at home anymore to be loyal to, so why not?

Yes, Tyler was corrupt, but he had his moments of professional responsibility, and this was one of them. He didn't like the idea of sitting back and letting hired killers come into his own county and town, no matter who they worked for. It went against his grain as a sworn enforcer of the law, but still he could live with hired killers if Ellison wanted that. What galled him was that it was Patrick Carrigan whom Ellison was so determined to kill. Tyler and Carrigan were hardly friends—Carrigan looked down on Tyler because of his well-known corruption—but, despite himself, Tyler had to admire Patrick Carrigan for the good man he was. He wished he had some notion of what Ellison had against Carrigan. Whatever it was, it was apparently serious business and had its roots in something years ago. He'd talked to Ellison enough to know that he and Carrigan had known each other when both were "young, free, careless men," as Ellison had put it.

Tyler entered the jail and went straight to the

coffee kettle boiling on the iron stove in the corner. He found his usual pewter cup, still stained with yesterday's coffee, and poured it full. The heat went right through the metal handle and burned his fingers, but Tyler was a tough man and hardly noticed it. He sipped the steaming brew with relish and headed toward the back, where the cells were.

One of his deputies, the one who had brought in Mickey Sparks, was emerging, looking extraordinarily tired.

"What's wrong with you, son?" asked Tyler.

"Been a long night, boss. A long night. Got me a colored boy in the back who I had figured to give me trouble, and I couldn't get no peace waiting for him to get around to causing it."

"Did he?"

"No. But more to the point of interest, there's two white fellows locked up beside him. Strangers. Look to be brothers."

"I heard about these fellows. I've been looking for somebody to show up."

"I know what you're thinking, boss, but I don't think this is them."

"Why not?"

"Well, odd as it sounds, it's because of the way they look. They look way too much like Patrick Carrigan to be men who've come to kill him."

"Look like him?"

"That's right, boss. They got to be kin of Carrigan's. Got to be."

"This all sounds right peculiar, son."

"It was a peculiar night last night. Maybe it was because of that ghost show. You ain't supposed to be summoning spirits and such. That's in the Bible. Maybe there's wicked spirits working in this town now because of that show."

"I hear that most such shows are really only tricks done with light and such. No real spirit-summoning going on."

"I don't know much about it. I just figure a man should be careful about such things."

The Carrigan brothers were awake and moving about in their cell when Tyler got to the back to meet them. They gazed at him, not sure who this newcomer was, and he looked back at them like a man who found them intriguing.

"Hello, gentlemen," he said at length, clicking a fingernail against the badge on his vest. "I'm the sheriff here. My name is Cordell Tyler."

"I'm Joseph Carrigan, and that there is my brother, Liam."

"Carrigan!"

"That's right. Nephews of Patrick Carrigan, the local rancher."

"You bear a striking resemblance to him. I noticed

it soon as I saw you, and my deputies had already mentioned it."

"That's what everybody's telling us. We've never met Patrick, so we'll have to see it for ourselves when we do."

"How is it you've never met your own uncle?"

"Because he came to this country from Ireland before my brother and I were born. We're native-born Irishmen. Our own father came over after Patrick years later and hoped to reunite with him, but it never happened. So for the last year or so, Liam and I have been tracking Patrick down, planning to meet him because he's all the family we've got left."

"You should know that he's a controversial man in this part of the territory."

"The controversy that we've heard about is that they say another rancher wants him killed. The story is he's hired two gunmen to do the job."

"I've heard the same. So I've been looking out for the arrival of two strangers."

"It isn't us, sheriff. I vow it before God. If we did anything regarding that situation, it would be to protect our uncle. Certainly not to hurt him."

"Why are you locked up here?"

Joseph gave the sheriff a greatly abbreviated and deliberately vague and compressed recounting of the prior night's events. "My brother is here only because he asked to be jailed with me, to keep an eye on me and make sure I was safe in here. As for me, I was in a row last night. I helped out a local woman being robbed by a man in an alley." He framed his next sentence carefully, determined not to reveal that it was Charlotte Canaday who had actually been involved in the wounding. "The robber wound up with a bullet in him, and I wound up here."

"Was he fatally shot?"

"No. Took a wound in the arm but nothing serious."

"Who was he?"

"A man named George Clifford, I was told."

"Clifford, eh? Well, he deserved it. He finds trouble everywhere he goes, then expects me and my deputies to leave him in peace just because he . . ." The sheriff trailed off, as if realizing he should not say what he was about to say.

"Go on, sheriff," Joseph said. "You were about to say that Clifford expects you to leave him alone because he works for Bret Ellison? Is that it?"

"No, no," Tyler said, the denial not very persuasive. "Why would that matter, who he works for?"

"The talk I hear all around since coming to this town is that it matters a lot. The talk is that you are an Ellison man yourself, sheriff. Bought and paid for."

Tyler's eyes narrowed, and he suddenly looked very fearsome. "A man on the side of the bars that you are should best learn how to control his tongue when he's talking to the man who has the key ring."

"I'm not saying it's true, sheriff, just that it's what people say. I'm a newcomer here. I don't know the truth of what goes on in Fire Creek."

"Well, all you need to know is to keep yourself out of this war between Ellison and Carrigan. Nothing good can come of involving yourself in it."

"Well, sir, I can tell you that we didn't come to Fire Creek to involve ourselves in anybody's conflicts. I can also tell you that the Carrigans believe strong in family, and what hurts the family involves all of us. We'll stay out of the war if we can, but if someone brings trouble to our uncle's doorstep, Liam and I will both be there to meet it."

"Amen," Liam said from further back in the cell.

The sheriff frowned at Joseph as if debating what he should say to him, then gave a little shrug and a shake of his head and apparently dismissed whatever lecture he'd been about to deliver.

"I'm letting you two go, on promise that you'll stay out of trouble," he said. "Visit your uncle, but don't get into his business or his problems. You be good, law-abiding men, and you'll have no trouble in Fire Creek."

"We are good, law-abiding men, sheriff, and so far all Fire Creek has given us is trouble."

"It happens sometimes. Now, get your boots on. I'm cutting you boys loose."

"That's it? We're free? No charges, no court-rooms, no trial?"

"I've got no reason to hold your brother, anyway, since he is here only because he volunteered to be. And if all you did was protect a woman from George Clifford, I have no inclination to make much of this. Clifford brings his own woes upon himself. This isn't the first time."

"Thank you, sheriff. I'll do my best to cause you no further reason to have to deal with me while I'm in Fire Creek."

"Make it a vow. Raise your right hands, both of you."

The brothers complied, though both thought it a silly gesture.

"Repeat: I vow that I shall give Sheriff Cordell Tyler no cause to regret that he set me free from in-carceration this day and will remain out of any trou-ble while in his jurisdiction."

They muttered the words together.

"You gents keep that vow, now. And most of all, stay out of the Fire Creek war."

CHAPTER SEVEN

Charlotte Canaday had walked all the way from Fire Creek to the Carrigan ranch house in the deepest late hours of the night, and when she was greeted at the door by Patrick Carrigan as Keefer Riley left, she was so weary that she nearly collapsed in his arms. He led her back to his office room and sat her on the sofa there. She looked up at him with hooded, bleary eyes, leaned over, and lay on her side. In moments, despite the news and the letter she had come to deliver, she was sound asleep. But a minute later, she stirred a little, opened her eyes again, and sat up, pulling from beneath her shawl a crumpled envelope, which she extended toward Carrigan. Her hand trembled, and her fingers lost their grip on it. The envelope fell to the floor as her head sank to the sofa again and her eyes closed once more.

Patrick eyed the envelope, the back side of which was turned up. He knelt and picked the envelope up and turned it over. His name was written on the front in a strong and familiar-looking hand, but he didn't recognize it at once.

The envelope had not been opened, as best he could tell. He opened it now, removed the letter inside, and began to read.

Dear Lord, it was a letter written to him by his own son, Patrick Junior, who had left this place many months before after an argument with his father! Patrick had been unsure what had become of his son since and prayed for him frequently. He read carefully, squinting his eyes and sometimes wiping away tears. Not all of what he read pleased him. Pat apparently was, at the time of writing, preparing to marry a young woman. The senior Carrigan was not glad to learn this, for the woman he wanted his son to marry was the one now sleeping on his sofa, still wearing the ring Pat had given her as a token of an engagement he now considered broken and defunct.

Patrick had looked forward to the day Charlotte Canaday would become Charlotte Carrigan, wife of his son, Pat. Even after Pat left and the engagement was broken, the father had retained hope that his son would eventually come to his senses and return to Charlotte.

Other portions of the letter, however, revealed news that Patrick was astonished to learn and quite pleased by. Pat wrote of having met two cousins, sons of his father's late brother, and described the help they had given him at great risk to themselves. These two brothers, Joseph and Liam Carrigan, were searching for Patrick, the letter said, wanting to meet in the flesh the uncle they had never known. He was sending the letter by them, he wrote.

The letter had a tone of friendly reconciliation, a son making peace with a father after a time of separation and hostility. The disputes that had divided him from his son had weighed on the mind of Patrick Carrigan for a long time now, and the letter gave him the luxury of yielding those burdens away, shrugging them off his shoulders. Pat was alive and well and, according to the letter, would come again to his father in due time, bringing his new bride with him.

Patrick folded the letter, put it back in its envelope, and laid it aside. Then he sat down in a comfortable chair on the other side of the room and watched Charlotte as she slept. A lovely, sweet young lady. He could almost wish she'd been around when he himself was a young, marriageable man. Now, if son Pat had indeed tied his life with that of another woman, she would never be his daughter-in-law. It made him sad.

Patrick, up for many hours, became drowsy, and his eyelids drooped. His mind continued to work, however, as sleep came on, and one realization struck that made him open his eyes wide again.

Pat had written that he had met two cousins,

sons of the brother of his own father, and was sending the letter to the Montana Territory by way of them. But the letter had been delivered to Patrick not by the two men Pat wrote about but by Charlotte. So somehow Charlotte must also have encountered this pair and gotten the letter from them. But how? And where?

Locally, surely. Charlotte had not been traveling of late, so she must have encountered these brothers in the immediate vicinity, so they were here, somewhere in or around Fire Creek. But if so, why had they passed the letter off to an intermediary to deliver? Why had they not simply ferreted out the location of his ranch and delivered it themselves?

Charlotte surely knew the answers, but he would not disturb her sleep just yet. Morning would provide an opportunity to talk.

Patrick shifted to a more comfortable position, rested his cheek against the padded side wing of his overstuffed chair, and let thoughts blank themselves away into the oblivion of dreamless sleep.

His next awareness was of a gentle hand brushing his whiskered cheek. He opened his eyes and looked up into the sweetly smiling face of Charlotte Canaday. But his eyes were drawn to something that seemed amiss about her, some odd fall of shadow across her face.

No, not shadow. As he looked more closely, he detected faint bruises along the side of her face. The hand that had brushed his face was bruised as well, along its back. And he also saw a rough abrasion on one of her wrists. He touched her hand and looked at her in concern.

"You are hurt, Charlotte."

"Not badly. I am fine."

"What happened?"

"I was accosted in an alley, by a robber who tried to take my ring."

He looked down at the ring on her left hand. She folded her fingers into a fist as if to display it more obviously. "Who?" he asked.

"Clifford . . . George Clifford."

"God! I'll kill the bastard!"

"He might kill you instead. Anyone associated with Ellison might kill you, Patrick. You are in danger every moment."

"That is nothing I don't know. But I'm tired of living in worry about it. I don't know what's true and what's false. Rumors of two strangers hired by Ellison to kill me, and then, when two strangers do show up, I'm told they bear a striking resemblance to me. Then I find a letter from my own son, telling me about two nephews I never knew I had, and how he's sending that letter by way of them because they're coming to find me. But instead of getting that letter from them, I get it from you." He smiled.

"I'm struggling to make sense of things right now, Charlotte."

"You found the letter, then."

"I did indeed. Did you read it, Charlotte?"

"No. No, I was tempted, because it was written by Pat, but it was addressed to you, and so I didn't."

"Well, I did read it."

"Is Pat well?"

"He is fine. There are things I'll tell you more about later. First, I want you to tell me how you got the letter."

"I got it from your nephew, a man named Joseph Carrigan. He is in Fire Creek, with his brother, Liam. They came here to find you."

"Yes, the letter tells me that. I didn't even know they existed. Or that my brother followed me to this country, or that he has since died."

"I'm very sorry to hear that."

"He was a good one. Better than me."

She squeezed his hand. "I doubt that is the case."

"Do my nephews really look like me?"

"Very much." She paused. "And I think they are good men, like you. Joseph came to my aid when Clifford robbed me. He leaped out of a hotel window onto a little porch roof, and his foot came right through the roof and clubbed Clifford in the head with his boot heel."

"No lie?"

"No lie."

"I'm quite impressed already. Where might I find this extraordinary man and his brother?"

She looked down. "There was a bit of a problem. I took Clifford's pistol from him, and after our first round of trouble was over, he came looking for it. I had to defend myself with it."

"You shot George Clifford?"

"Not all that badly. Just a minor wound."

Patrick looked at her with an expression of admiring awe, then slowly laughed. "I salute you, girl. May God bless and prosper any lass who shoots a hole into such a piece of rubbish as an Ellison man."

She stood up straight and turned away, putting distance between herself and him. Emotions threatening to rise, she looked at him fiercely. "I must make a demand on you," she said. "I must know the origins of this trouble between you and Ellison. For I see things coming that fill me with dread, bad things, for you, for me, for Pat, and for these lost nephews of yours should they ally themselves with you."

"Why do you see these grim things on their way?"

"Because of you, Patrick. Because it seems that everyone around you, everyone whose life entwines with yours, finds trouble and division. Have you not noticed this? You war with Ellison, for whatever cause, yet you also war with your own son, who had to leave here to find peace. I have been your friend, and very nearly your own daughter-in-law, and for that association I find myself robbed and bothered by those who align themselves with your enemies. And now, your two nephews come to find you, and before they are a full day in your town, they find themselves afoul of your enemy's law and cast into jail."

"Jail, you say?"

"Yes indeed, Patrick. Joseph is a noble man, and he took the blame for shooting Clifford so that I could stay out of trouble. But he himself was jailed for it, and his brother had himself jailed with him, simply because they are brothers."

At this, Patrick's eyes lighted, and his Irish brogue heightened again. "Aye, brothers. It is as it should be with brothers, one to stand by the other." He held up the letter. "In this letter, my own son tells me how my brother, God rest him, followed me to this land and brought with him his two sons—Joseph and Liam, named after our grandfathers on both sides of our family—because I was his brother and it was right for him to follow me. But he did not find me and instead made a life for himself and his sons in Tennessee, living there until he died. The war divided his sons, one going one way, one the other, but after they came again together, as brothers. Family is supreme . . . all else, all other allegiances, must give way before the bonds of blood." He grinned broadly. "I want to meet these fine nephews of mine. I shall go see them in the very jail itself, if that is where they are."

She shook her head firmly. "Patrick, no, no, it would be a mad thing for you to do. The sheriff is Ellison's man, and it is there his allegiances lie. If you walk into that jail, you will find yourself occupying a cell there."

He gave a small grimace. "Perhaps that is as it should be. My nephews come to find me and find imprisonment. If the same should happen to me, perhaps that is as it should be as well."

"Please, Patrick, no. I lost your son, and now must I lose you as well?"

"I don't know, Charlotte. I don't know."

"You have not yet answered the question I put to you. What is the origin of the trouble between you and Ellison? I must know, Patrick. I must."

He drew in a long breath, slowly, and let it out more slowly yet. "There are things a man does not wish to speak of . . . things best left to his own knowledge alone. There are matters between Ellison and myself that are of such a character. Naught would be gained by me telling you of them."

"But why, Patrick? Why?"

"I cannot tell you. Enough questions! I'll now go to Fire Creek and meet these nephews who have come so far to see me."

"I fear for you, Patrick."

"I shall be careful. I shall never suffer the likes of Ellison to end my days."

"You vow it to me, Patrick?"

"I vow it."

Unable to believe their bout with the law had come to such an unexpected easy conclusion, Joseph and Liam headed first to breakfast at a café, then to their hotel for their goods. Both had decided that their inability to find out precisely where they could locate Patrick Carrigan's ranch would not be allowed to become a lasting impediment. The man was a well-known local figure, involved in the cattlemen's association and known, apparently, to everyone in town. Someone, somewhere, would tell them where to find him.

Most of the work at the local livery was done by a small-framed black boy named Leonard Smart. The Carrigan brothers had met him when they put their horses into stable, and he greeted him at the big double doorway when they walked in to reclaim their mounts.

"Hello, gentlemen," he said in his clear, slightly high voice. Joseph smiled at the boy, noticing again something he had commented about to Liam earlier: Leonard had almost no trace of the accent typical of most black individuals they had known. Clearly, he had worked on ridding himself of it. Joseph decided to be forthright and ask him about it.

"Yes, sir, I have worked hard to make sure I speak well," he said. "My father taught me to do that. He said a man can go much farther if he speaks well . . . and so far I've found that to be true."

Joseph glanced around the dirty, dank livery. It didn't look like a particularly high climb to him. But Leonard was only a boy, after all, and probably it was a fine achievement to have responsibility for day-to-day operation of a livery stable.

"I'm sure you'll do well all through your life," Joseph said. "You'll climb high."

"I intend to do the best I can, sir."

"You can start by fetching our horses," said Liam. Joseph gave him a harsh glance, thinking his tone with Leonard was somewhat rude.

He engaged the boy in conversation again when he brought out the horses. "We're looking for a local man. Perhaps you can tell us where to find him."

Leonard cocked up one brow, an act that made him look older than his years. "Might you be looking for Mr. Patrick Carrigan?"

"Perhaps so. How did you know that?"

"Just a guess, sir, based on your appearance. You bear a strong resemblance."

"His late brother was our father," Joseph said.

"I believe it, sir. You look much like him, and him there with you looks even more so."

"We'd like to find him. We've come a long way to see him."

"I can tell you where his ranch is."

"And you're willing to do that, no questions asked?" Liam said.

"Why wouldn't I be, sir?"

Liam hesitated, unsure whether he should bring up the now-familiar matter of the rumored hired killers. But he'd knocked on that door, and now he had to answer it.

"Because there are stories around town that someone has bad intentions for our uncle and has hired a couple of men to do harm to him."

"More than do harm, sir. The story is that they've been hired to kill him." He paused. "But I know it isn't you gentlemen."

"Simply because we resemble him?"

"That, partly, but mostly because I know who the real hired killers are."

Joseph and Liam gaped at the boy, then looked at each other, unable to find words.

"How do you know that?" Joseph asked.

"I figured it out, sir. Just figured it out." He paused. "That's their horses over there, in those two stalls."

"Damn!" Liam exclaimed.

Joseph put his hand on Leonard's shoulder. "How did you figure it out?"

"I just did. I just reasoned it out."

"But how? You can't just assume that because two strangers showed up in town, they're hired killers. That's what people have been thinking about us, and they're wrong. You could be wrong, too."

"I don't think so, sir. Not with what I've seen."

"And what is that?"

"I saw them getting into town. They came in on the train, with their horses in the stable car. Two big, tall men, faces all dark and grim, dressed in black clothes like preachers. But they had big pistols strapped to them, and they carried luggage that included a couple of long cases—rifle cases, I believe."

"Well, it sounds suspicious, but I'm not sure you can know from that alone that they are what you think they are."

"No, sir, but there's more than that. I heard them talking to each other when they brought in their horses. Talking about Patrick Carrigan and how to find him."

Liam said, "Well, that does sound incriminating to me."

"Where are these two men staying?"

"At the Arms, I think. But I don't know that."

"Have you seen them since they left their horses here?"

"No, sir. Well, I did see one of them, walking down the boardwalk on the other side of the street there. He was heading for Mrs. O'Tell's place."

"What place is that?"

"Mrs. O'Tell's . . . you don't know about it?"

"Not a thing," Joseph replied.

"Well, it's a bad place . . . bad women there. You know what I'm trying to say."

"I regret I didn't learn of that place earlier," Liam said.

"Don't listen to him, he's a sinful-minded man," Joseph said.

"There's a lot of sinful men about," Leonard said. "They mostly wind up over at Mrs. O'Tell's when they're in Fire Creek."

"Would this Mrs. O'Tell be able to guide Liam and me to these two men?"

"Mrs. O'Tell won't do it, sir. She won't ever betray anyone who does business with her women. It's her notion of honor, you see."

"Good to know that even sporting women have some sense of honor," Joseph said.

"Why, sporting women are among some of the finest human beings I've ever known," Liam said. "In the usual sense or the biblical sense, either one."

Joseph said, "Leonard, do you know when these two are coming back for these horses?"

"No, sir. They didn't put no outer limit on how

long the horses would be stabled. So it could be a long time"—his eyes shifted past the brothers and out the double doors—"or they could come get them right now."

"No, no, it's Joseph and me who are getting our horses right now," Liam said. "We're the good ones, remember?"

"Wait, Liam," Joseph said, following Leonard's gaze and looking back over his shoulder. "Leonard's right. There are two men coming toward the livery right now."

Liam looked. "That them, Leonard?"

"That's them, sir."

"Liam and I are going to step behind that stall wall over there, and if you'd kindly not mention that we're here, it might be helpful to us in making sure our uncle is protected. You want that, don't you?"

"Yes, sir. Mr. Patrick is a fine and good man, sirs. He's always been good to me and to my family."

"That's good to hear."

"I'll not reveal you, gentlemen. I'll not let on that anybody else is here."

"But somebody else is," said a voice from within one of the nearby stalls. Joseph and Liam wheeled, utterly startled.

From the shadows of the stall, a figure appeared, stepping into the stall doorway. Joseph froze, surprised to see Mickey Sparks materializing in the murk almost like one of Professor Marvel's projected phantoms.

"Mickey, how long have you been there?" Liam asked.

"For a spell. You'd best step in here quick, unless you want them two to see you," Sparks replied, glancing toward the door and the advancing figures of the two purported hired killers.

Liam grabbed Joseph's arm and pulled him toward the stall. Sparks withdrew back into the darkness, and the Carrigan brothers went after him, closing the stall door behind them.

Two shadows darkened the big square of light that was the open double door of the livery. With only the faintest lingering glance at the stall that hid the brothers and Mickey Sparks, Leonard the livery boy turned to greet his two newest customers.

"Good day, gentlemen," he said. "How may I assist you?"

"Well, boy, how do you think? We need our horses."

"Very well, gentlemen. I'll have them ready for you quickly."

"Fine . . . but if you're looking for a gratuity, boy, you can get that out of your black head. We're ministers of the gospel, and we don't consider ourselves obliged to pay money out for special favors."

"No," said the second man. "It should be the pleasure of every person to assist those who are doing God's work and to expect nothing in return for it."

Liam, Joseph, and Sparks exchanged puzzled looks in the stall. Ministers? Maybe these men weren't who they assumed they were after all. Misidentification would be easy. Liam and Joseph knew that from their own experience in Fire Creek so far.

Leonard set about his work, getting out the horses and saddling them. They were already rubbed down and brushed. Leonard had taken care of that early on. The two strangers paced about the livery, lighting up cigars. The smoke smelled strong and drifted directly toward the stall that hid the brothers and Sparks. Joseph covered his nose. He didn't mind the smell of cigars—Liam smoked quite a few of them—but sometimes they made him sneeze, something he really didn't want right now.

Although, he pondered, maybe it was foolish to be hiding. If these men were merely traveling preachers, something they certainly looked as if they could be, there was no reason to hide.

But something was amiss with them, and Joseph had to think a minute to figure out what it was. Most Protestant ministers he'd run across, particularly the missionary-minded itinerants such as these seemed to be, weren't typically cigar-smoking types. Joseph looked over at Liam, who was frowning and perhaps thinking something similar, because he gave his head a quick shake as if to indicate that something was not right here.

While Leonard worked on getting the horses ready, the two "preachers" milled about, until one of them stubbed his toe on a block of wood lying about and let out a very unministerial curse, loudly.

Peering through a crack in the stall door, Liam watched as the other "minister" gave the cursing one an angry look in response to the curse.

Leonard led one of the horses out. "Did you say something, sir?" he asked the curser.

"Me? No, boy. Nothing." He paused. "But you can, maybe, help me out with some information. Reverend Campbell and myself are in need of finding a particular rancher of these parts, a man we are informed desires spiritual counsel."

"Yes," said the other man. "He wants to make sure he goes to heaven . . . and we want to help him get there."

"His name," said the first, "is Carrigan. Patrick Carrigan."

That was it, to Liam, the final answer to the question. Leonard had been right: these *were* the rumored hired killers. Had to be. He hadn't missed the grim, twisted meaning in what had just been said.

"Sir, I don't know this Mr. Carrigan."

"Bosh, boy! How ignorant a darky are you, anyway? This man, we are told, is quite a noted and well-known cattleman. How could you work in a livery and not know the locals? Don't try to lie to us, boy. Liars go to hell, you know."

"So do murderers, sir."

"Murderers? What the hell are you talking about? We're preachers."

"Preachers don't generally say 'what the hell,' sir. Nor do they spend time at houses of sin like Mrs. O'Tell's place . . . where I saw you going in the door with my own eyes."

"You got a sharp tongue for a damned darky, boy. And you don't even talk right for a darky! I never heard such smooth-sounding a voice come out of a negro. I don't like the way that sounds."

"I merely talk as I talk, sir."

It didn't seem to Liam that Leonard intended that statement to come out sounding glib and patronizing, but somehow it did. And the bigger of the two "preachers" reacted strongly to the perceived insolence. Because of the angle of his limited view through the hole in the stall, Liam could not see what happened, but the loud, ringing, flesh-on-flesh crack of a hand on Leonard's face was unmistakable. Then, as Liam watched, Leonard stumbled into his view, face twisted in pain. He'd literally been knocked into a stagger by the blow. He tripped over the same piece of wood against which one of the "preachers" had stubbed his toe and fell right against the door of the stall behind which the Carrigan brothers and Mickey Sparks hid.

The noise he made bumping into the door startled Mickey Sparks, who moved and lost his balance, accidentally knocking his hand against the stall wall with a loud *thump*. Liam glared at him, and Joseph winced.

"What the hell was that?" one of the men outside said.

It all happened fast from that point on. "Campbell" came toward the stall as Leonard struggled back to his feet and dodged to the side. The Carrigan brothers and Sparks crouched lower, then the absurdity of trying to continue to hide became clear, particularly to Liam, and he readied himself and lunged up just as Campbell thrust his head over the top of the stall door and looked inside. Liam came up fist-first, pounding Campbell in the jaw so hard he fell backward, tripped over his own feet, and came down hard on his rump. Liam felt quite a sense of satisfaction. No one would knock about a mere boy like Leonard, not while he was around to stop it!

Liam yanked open the stall door and emerged, Sparks right after him and Joseph coming out last. Leonard was nearby, leaning on a stable support beam, blood coming from his lip. Campbell was getting up clumsily, groping at his jaw. Liam headed straight for him and let go with a swinging kick. His boot toe hit Campbell just under the chin and sent him flopping back. The other "preacher," name unknown, was so astonished by the attack of the little army from the stall that he stood transfixed, mouth agape.

Campbell proved to be as tough as a knotted oak. Rising with remarkable strength given the fierce kick he'd just taken, Campbell moved toward Liam with a face burning like an overheated furnace. Liam reacted defensively, putting up his arms as Campbell took a swing at him. The blow connected, but because Campbell was disoriented from Liam's kick, his fist skidded off without taking full effect.

Liam waded in, his own fist firing out like the impact end of a battering ram, and Campbell's chin took another hit. Campbell staggered backward, then somehow got hold of himself and charged again. This time, his fist hit Liam squarely on the right side of his face, rocking him effectively. Liam let out a grunt and did some staggering of his own, but he, too, was a tough oak and came back to inflict damage again on Campbell. The pair, seemingly evenly matched, traded blows for two minutes as the others circled and weaved around them. Joseph, not by nature as violent as his brother, thought of intervening but found no good opportunity. But his situation changed when the other "preacher" took a lead from his partner and struck Joseph on the face just as Campbell had struck Liam.

The blow only served to jolt Joseph into a keen, concentrated awareness and stirred anger in him as well. "Kill my uncle . . . is that your notion?" he said loudly, lighting into his attacker with gusto. "You want to send him to paradise? I don't think so, 'preacher,' I don't think so."

Joseph fought hard, but his opponent was swift and seemed able to anticipate Joseph's blows before they fell. He was a capable dodger, keeping Joseph dancing, constantly aiming and reaiming his blows, never connecting as well as he hoped. Meanwhile, Liam and Campbell did a similar, if less lively, dance of violence. Watching it all were Leonard and Sparks, the former nearly frozen in fear, huddled back against the livery wall, the latter tense as a wire, muscles twitching, fists clinched and ready to strike . . . but there was no opponent for Sparks.

Inevitably, the two sets of fighters began to get in each other's way, Campbell backing into his partner by accident and almost knocking him down and Liam actually landing one blow on Joseph's shoulder, causing Joseph to yell loudly in pain. An earlier hand injury also took its toll on Joseph, causing him to lighten the force of his punches, giving his opponent a steadily growing advantage.

CHAPTER EIGHT

The fight, hidden as it was within the walls of the livery, nevertheless caused some noise and drew some attention from people who passed outside at angles that gave them a view through the open doors. The fighters gradually worked their way toward those doors, not by plan but by the simple, random path of their movements. As minutes passed, a small crowd of onlookers gathered in the street near the livery doors to watch this unexpected show.

Among the onlookers was Loretta Abernathy, who had made a show of herself during Professor Marvel's ghost performance. She watched in disgust as the two strangers she'd first seen at Marvel's show slugged it out with two other men she had never seen before.

She wouldn't abide this, not in her town! Fire Creek had always been a peaceful place, and now it seemed to be changing. Everywhere she turned, she encountered rumors of hired killers and frightening talk of the inexplicable hostilities between ranchers Bret Ellison and Patrick Carrigan. It seemed anymore that such things cast an ever-present pall over a town she had loved for years. People even talked of the "Fire Creek war" these days—*war!* It was unbelievable, intolerable.

She watched the fight for only a couple of minutes. It seemed to her that the pair whose looks reminded her of Patrick Carrigan were holding their own and slowly prevailing. She edged up to a man who was also watching the fight.

"Who are the ones in the dark suits, Mr. Waller?" she asked him.

"I don't know for sure, Loretta. I heard somebody saying they think they are traveling preachers coming through."

That was all it took for Loretta Abernathy. She'd not simply stand and watch while men of God were abused by strangers in her own town. The big woman wheeled and stomped to the office of Sheriff Cordell Tyler.

"Fighting, did you say, Loretta?" he said. "Knives, guns, fists, what?"

"Fists is what I saw. But you never know how far it will go."

"I'll go put an end to it."

Tyler's approach caused the little but growing

crowd of onlookers to break apart. He passed through the midst of the people and walked boldly right up to the fighting men, drew his pistol, and fired it into the sky. The blast got the attention of the fighters and brought the brawl to a halt, at least momentarily.

"Well, Mr. Joseph Carrigan," Tyler said to Joseph. "I thought you and I had a firm agreement when I turned you loose. You would avoid trouble. But now, only a short time later, I find you brawling like a common drunkard in the livery stable."

"I was forced to it," Joseph said. "I didn't want to fight."

"But you did . . . you did . . . and after you'd vowed to me you'd keep out of trouble."

"I was struck in the face, sheriff. Tell me the truth. If you were struck in the face without provocation, would you stand for it? Or would you fight?"

"It depended on whether I wanted to go to jail or not."

"Jail?"

"Hell yes, jail. That's where public brawlers go in my town."

"What about hired murderers?"

"What are you talking about?"

"These two!" Joseph bellowed, waving at the two men in black.

"So these are hired murderers? Who have they murdered?"

"Nobody, that I know of," Joseph said. "But they plan to. They plan to kill our uncle, Patrick Carrigan."

"Oh! Those damned rumors again! Now, how do you know these men are these widely anticipated assassins?"

"Because we heard the things they said to each other," Liam threw in. "They claim to be preachers, of all things, then talk of their goal to make sure that Patrick Carrigan gets sent to heaven. I know what they meant by that . . . and if these two are preachers, I'm the president of these United States."

"Well, they look like they could be preachers to me. And maybe all they want to do is save Patrick Carrigan's soul."

"Why his in particular? Why not yours, sheriff? Or mine?"

"We care about the welfare of all souls," threw in one of the men in black. "But we have heard that this Patrick Carrigan is a man who might be in danger, and some who care about what becomes of him asked us to come to this place and find him. And so we are here."

"Sounds believable to me," said the sheriff. "Now, you Carrigans, you're coming with me. Clearly, I let you go far too early."

"You're putting us under arrest?" Joseph asked.

"I am indeed," Tyler replied.

"Hell . . . I ain't going," Liam said.

"I believe you are."

The voice that said those words came from behind Liam, and he pivoted to see one of Tyler's deputies there, pistol drawn and aimed at his midsection. Liam froze, stunned.

A second deputy, drawn by the crowd, showed up and involved himself. "What about this one, sheriff?" he asked, pointing at Mickey Sparks, who lingered in the doorway of the livery, standing near Leonard.

"He wasn't involved in any fighting," Joseph said.

"Maybe not, but he was here, and that's enough. He's going back, too. When I turn men loose and they get right into a public brawl, I don't look the other way."

Liam and Joseph ended up in the same cell they had vacated earlier, Mickey Sparks beside them again, as before. But this time, Mickey was not alone. After he'd been evicted that morning, a deputy had made another arrest, and that man, a scrawny, stringy scrap of a man who introduced himself as Rambling Jim Murphy, was in Mickey's old cell when Mickey was shoved back into it. There were no other jail occupants at the moment beyond Sparks, the Carrigans, and Murphy.

"Sorry to have to stick you with a colored fellow,

Rambling Jim," said the sheriff as he locked up Sparks. Clearly, Rambling Jim was no stranger to Tyler, and probably not to this jail.

"Why, I don't mind it," Rambling Jim said. "I figure that when the good Lord shakes things out at the end of time, we'll all learn that a man is a man is a man, none of us different except on the outside."

Hearing this in the next cell, Joseph said to Liam, "That man in there is wiser than most, I think."

Tyler shook his head. "Be that as it may, Rambling Jim, it always galls me to have to lock up a colored man and a white one together. The Creator surely didn't intend for a white man to have to live together with a black one in a way like that. That black skin is the mark of Cain, you know."

"I've heard that said in pulpits," Rambling Jim replied. "Never heard it proved, though. Ain't no scripture to back it that I'm aware of."

"I'll never figure you out, Jim," said Tyler. "You stay in trouble most of the time, drinking and fighting and gambling your life away, such as it is, but you know the Bible better than any man I've run across."

"I know it, but I find it hard to live by. It's danged difficult, sheriff."

"I know. I know, Jim. Listen, this darky cause you any problem, you holler for me or one of my men. We'll take care of it for you."

"I'll cause no one any problems, sheriff," said Sparks. "I'm a decent and law-abiding man. And I've done nothing to justify being thrown back in here."

"You were found in the company of brawlers," the sheriff replied. "Maybe you'd be better off not keeping company with Irish." Tyler glanced toward Liam and Joseph's cell.

"Now, Mr. Tyler, you're beginning to offend me," said Murphy, glaring.

Tyler ignored him. "You men settle yourselves down while I go up front and talk to our visiting preachers to find out what went on. I'll be back to talk to you again later."

Watching the sheriff disappear through the heavy door that separated the cell area from the front office, Liam shook his head. "That bastard already has his mind made up," he said. "He believes those men in the black suits really are preachers. He's taking them at their word."

"He knows better, really," Joseph said. "The problem is that he's bought by this Ellison fellow. There's no fouler sinner than a corrupt lawman."

"Preach it, Joseph," Liam said. "Amen!"

"I'd like to meet Ellison," Joseph went on. "I'd like the chance to talk to him and find out what in the devil he has against our uncle."

"Hell, I'd like just to meet our uncle!" Liam

replied. "If we can ever get out of this jail and find somebody who knows where he resides, maybe we'll get the chance."

"Who is your uncle?" asked Rambling Jim through the intercell window.

"A local rancher named Patrick Carrigan," Liam answered.

"You've not met him before?"

"Never. It's a long story."

"You need somebody to show you where he can be found, I can do that. I know the man and at one time built a shed for him. I'm a carpenter, you see, a traveling carpenter. Rambling Jim Murphy."

"We'll take you up on your offer, Rambling Jim. We thank you. How well do you know him?"

"Reasonably well."

"Do you know Bret Ellison?"

"I do. I worked for him, too. Added a room to his house in the fort."

"Fort? He has a fort?"

"An old army fort, now abandoned and passed on to Ellison."

Liam frowned in puzzlement. "How does a man persuade the government to give him one of its old army forts?"

"It's called influence and power, Mr. Carrigan. And money. Ellison has got it all. Him having that fort proves it. He lives in the house inside that used to be that of the commanding officer. A fine place, quite fine. Stockade all around it."

"A man who lives in a fort must be hiding from something," Joseph observed.

Liam asked, "Rambling Jim, do you know the cause of the difficulties between our uncle and Bret Ellison?"

The man seemed hesitant to reply. At length, he said, "There were some things said regarding that while I was working for Ellison. He found out I'd worked for your uncle, and that set him off."

"What did you learn?"

"Not much . . . just that it goes way back, back a very long ways in their lives. Back to something that happened in Missouri, I think it was."

"What?"

"It involved a woman, I believe. The woman Ellison married later on. She's dead now, but her portrait hangs above his mantelpiece, and they say he ends each day by staring at it and talking to her until he's too tired to talk anymore."

"Woman trouble . . . no worse kind for bringing out the worst in men," Liam said. "Maybe Patrick and Ellison were after the same woman, and that caused the resentment."

"That's not it," said Rambling Jim. "There's something more to it, something that neither of them seems willing to talk much about, not that I know of.

All Ellison would say on it was that he holds Patrick Carrigan responsible for the biggest loss in his life. And that he'll never forgive what was done."

"Biggest loss . . . money? Land?"

"I can only think he means his woman. The loss of his wife."

"How would Patrick be responsible for that?"

"I don't know. But if you could find out that answer, you might then understand what lies behind the war at Fire Creek."

Keefer Riley grimaced and halted his horse. He climbed down slowly and stretched his muscles, gripping his sides and massaging around toward his spine. His back ached terribly, an affliction growing more frequent the older he grew. Blast it all! He'd been what he was, a cattleman, all his adult life. And now he was growing too sore-jointed and achy and creaky and old to keep up the necessary pace.

He'd have to give it up soon and find some other way to make a living that didn't put so much strain on him. Running a shop, maybe.

God, but he'd hate to give up the life he'd always known! He couldn't imagine doing anything other than what he'd known for so many years. But as he stretched again, twisting his spine right and left and right, and pondered what he was doing right now, he realized that there might be aspects of change that would be welcome.

For the past seven months, his life had not really been the one he'd loved so well. The Fire Creek war, this absurd, unending, and publicly undefined dispute between Ellison and Carrigan, had changed everything. And it was growing worse the more time went by. At first, it was vague talk, imprecise threats, a general sense of tension, and an unwillingness on Patrick's part to talk much about anything to do with Ellison. It was merely odd then, especially in that Patrick had initially had a hospitable attitude toward Bret Ellison, speaking of him almost fondly and noting that they had known each other when they were young. Then things had changed, deteriorating in an accelerating fashion, Patrick growing unwilling to talk about Ellison at all. Then, suddenly, he was talking again, at least some, but always emphasizing that Ellison was dangerous and wicked, someone anyone associated with the Carrigan ranch should be careful of and avoid.

Riley dismissed the changes in Patrick Carrigan as mere oddities, probably unexplainable and likely to alter themselves again later on. Perhaps the man was going through some sort of personal crisis, distorting his judgment. Then something else happened: an attack by two of Ellison's cowboys upon one employed by Carrigan. It had taken place on a remote road, no one about, and, according to the victim, who had been beaten so badly he'd been unable to remount his horse and ride home but had managed to crawl and drag himself to a house about a mile away, the men who had beaten him had told him to deliver a message to Patrick Carrigan: Ellison had declared war on him, and "old debts would be paid." And from there on, matters had worsened, occasional shots being fired at Carrigan employees— one of them wounded, in fact, by a shot that took off a piece of the left side of his neck—and word eventually reached the Carrigan spread that Bret Ellison intended to see Patrick Carrigan in his grave.

It was hard to believe at first, but Ellison's ranch hands had become hostile and violent toward Carrigan's whenever they met. It quickly grew clear that Bret Ellison's hatred of Patrick Carrigan was being generalized to include anyone associated with Carrigan. When shots began being fired toward Carrigan men, the seriousness of the danger was obvious to all. Inevitably, word leaked out to the public at large, and the Fire Creek war became the talk of the local populace.

Generally, sentiment was in favor of Carrigan, whose reputation was that of a friendly, generous, down-to-earth man, whereas Ellison was aloof, conceited, overly powerful, and with a tendency to seek to use that power, and his substantial "old money" wealth, to ensure that he and his always had their way. This trait did not set well with the earthy people of Montana, most of whom had little in common with the aristocratic Ellison.

It was also widely believed—rightly, in Riley's view—that Ellison controlled the local law. His influence at higher levels of government was already evident through his possession of what had been government property, the old stockaded military fort formerly called Fort Greene, now informally termed Fort Ellison.

Riley twisted his back again, then bent slowly, straight-spined, to touch his toes, stretching the aching muscles in the small of his back. He rose slowly, sighing, and swung back into the saddle. Turning his horse, he began riding slowly toward Fire Creek again.

He wasn't sure how best to fulfill the assignment that Patrick had given him. Patrick had told him to learn more about the two strangers who had showed up at the ghost show and "find out if they're worth being afraid of." How could he go about that? He wasn't likely to get much help from the local law.

The terrain grew more rugged as he neared Fire Creek—which was the name of a stream as well as the town. The road took a turn around the side of a wooded hill, and as soon as he rode out into the clear again, Riley's instincts gave him a warning. Something was wrong . . . he just knew it.

At that moment, his horse stumbled, and, ironically, that saved him. The horse staggered to one side and made a dip, so that Riley's head was lower than it would have been otherwise, and the rifle slug that fired out of the creekside grove sailed off harmlessly above his head.

His horse righted itself again, and he spurred it into a run, circling off the road and into a somewhat overgrown area, allowing him some cover behind trees. He saw a big knoll of boulders and took his horse behind it, where he dismounted, tied off the horse, and from the boot on its saddle removed his faithful Henry rifle. He circled around the rocks and back in among the trees and, as he had hoped he would, saw movement in the grove across the road.

It was just a flash among the trees but a revealing one. He saw a man's arm and shoulder, a familiar slouch hat, and a glimpse of a face. Rex Oliver, his own counterpart at the Ellison spread. This did not much surprise him. Oliver was a foul fellow, brutish and mean, with a known criminal record. He'd reportedly robbed several freight stations and one bank and boasted to friends of having killed a freight station clerk who dared to try to stop him from one of his robberies.

Riley swore beneath his breath and vowed to himself that this attempted murder would not go un-avenged. Oliver would not leave that grove of trees alive. Riley dodged behind a tree and raised and le-vered the Henry.

Blast! Oliver had seen him. He could tell by the way the man moved in the grove, ducking low, then peering out for a moment through a gap in the nee-dles. Riley took aim down the long Henry barrel and saw that Oliver was in turn aiming back at him.

Riley fired without hesitation. He'd already been shot at once, so he had every moral right to defend himself.

But at the same moment as he squeezed the trig-ger, Oliver did the same. Riley saw the flash and pow-der burst, obliterating for a moment his own view of Oliver. But when the smoke cleared, he saw Oliver no more. The man had fallen back.

Had he hit him? Riley waited a moment, then saw movement. Oliver was rising, coming fully to his feet.

He staggered out of the grove, blood streaming from a hole at the base of his neck on the right side. He still had his rifle, but it fell from nerveless fingers, which then groped up toward the wound. Riley le-vered his Henry in case he had to use it again, but at this point, Oliver did not look to be a threat. The man trembled, bled, staggered, then tripped on his own feet and fell to the side, thudding against the ground. He moved a little, then grew still.

Riley stared, hardly believing what he'd just done. He'd killed a man. It was justified, of course, but still stunning to consider. And even though he'd not liked Oliver—despised him, in fact—he'd still known him, and it was odd to consider that he was dead by Riley's own bullet.

Riley stood slowly and walked out to the road, staring at the dead body. Then he noticed something odd in how he felt. Fighting a burst of dizziness, he looked down at himself and gasped.

His shirt was drenched in blood. Blood so abundant it began to drip from his sodden shirt onto his trousers and boots. He felt nauseated and began to tremble. He felt gingerly along himself with a hand growing numb and found that he was shot in nearly the same place Oliver had been shot.

The irony hurt even if the wound did not. And it did not hurt; he'd not even been aware when the bullet struck him, indicating it had probably hit him just as his own rifle recoiled against his shoulder, masking the impact of the bullet.

Feeling weaker by the moment, he turned to go back to find his hidden horse and get back on the road again. He needed help, fast. He was losing a good deal of blood, and he felt weaker and sicker by the moment. And now the wound was beginning to ache dully, the pain radiating out to his shoulders and chest and up into his head.

He was on the verge of fainting by the time he reached his horse, and it took almost all his energy to loose it and mount up. Leaning forward in the saddle, he fought off a great wave of sickness and began riding back through the trees and to the road.

He wasn't sure he would be able to remain conscious long enough to reach the town of Fire Creek. He prayed that his horse, which had made this journey many times, would make it again without guidance. And that he would somehow manage to remain in the saddle even without his senses.

It all became a moot issue, however, when he reached the road and noted, in what remained of his consciousness, that something had changed. Oliver's body no longer lay on the road. Where it had been was a puddle of fresh blood, congealing in the dust, but no Oliver.

Who could have taken his corpse, and how so quickly? Curiosity made him force his body upright in the saddle. He managed to clear his head and his eyes long enough to look around . . . and he saw him then, Oliver himself, not dead at all but standing up, leaning on a tree with an empty holster around his waist. Empty because he held the pistol in his hand.

Two things filled Riley's addled, muddy mind at that moment: a sense of horror at the realization that Oliver was still alive and dangerous and a sense of being back at that ghost show again, this time seeing a real ghost, a *real* being back from the dead. No optical frauds this time. Oliver had somehow come back.

That thought was his last. A new wave of weakness struck him, and he lurched forward in the saddle again, unwittingly tugging at the reins and causing the horse to turn toward Oliver. His vision starting to fail, Riley blinked at the figure slumped against the tree and watched as Oliver's trembling arm managed to raise the pistol a little straighter and aim it a little truer.

Riley passed out just in time to miss any awareness of the pistol going off. He did not see the flash or hear the blast or feel the bullet tear into his chest. When he tilted out of the saddle and was dumped onto the ground, he had no awareness of it.

His horse paused, turned, sniffed at his supine form, then moved on, stepping along toward Fire Creek. Riley made a faint moaning noise, his chest shuddered through three more slow breaths, then quivered to stillness, and he breathed no more.

Oliver, lungs wheezing and his own strength now almost gone, pushed away from his tree and staggered toward the road. He had to know, simply had to know, that Riley was dead.

He made it to the body on the road and looked down. His vision shimmered, light patterns dancing across his field of vision, but he was able to see that

Riley truly was not breathing. His eyes were half open, going glassy, staring into the sky, and when the sun came out from behind a cloud and beamed down into his face and eyes, the lids did not flutter closed. The man was dead.

Oliver managed a smile. He'd done it. He'd killed Patrick Carrigan's right-hand man. At the cost of his own life, maybe, but still he'd done it.

Bret Ellison would be proud of him. He smiled again, and now his vision was nothing but a white blank that slowly turned dark. He staggered, pivoted, lost his balance, and fell, landing partly atop the body of Keefer Riley, dying there with his own form touching the body of the man he had killed as the final act of his own life.

CHAPTER NINE

There had been a time when Patrick Carrigan enjoyed nothing more than making the ride from his ranch into Fire Creek. It was a pleasant, scenic journey, and the road was easy.

Now, everything was different. He could not pass a tree or a boulder along the way without an impulse to cringe and hide. These were dangerous days to be Patrick Carrigan. Even his men were being shot at, out on the range as they worked.

Damn Bret Ellison! The man was making his life a misery. And eventually, Patrick was nearly certain, Ellison would bring his life to an end.

There were times when Patrick had considered ending his own life before Ellison got the opportunity. It was not that he hated living; in fact, he loved life. It was simply that the impetus behind Ellison's punishment of him would not be one that would fade with time. If it were subject to fading, it would have done so already.

Worst of all, Patrick, in his most objective moments, actually could understand why Ellison was so hateful and even violence-prone. Had their roles been reversed, Patrick himself might be just as determined to see Ellison brought down as Ellison was now determined to see *him* destroyed.

Making it even more difficult for Patrick was that he did not feel free to discuss the situation in any detail with others. His men, his professional associates, his friends—all ached to know what was at the root of the war between the two ranchers, yet Patrick could not tell them. He longed to be free of this intensely private burden, yet he dreaded the thought of the truth being known.

And so he continued to hide it, and more and more to hide himself. That was the attraction of the old line camp he'd talked to Keefer Riley about going to: it was private, a place he could exist without any general knowledge of his presence there. Whether he would truly be safer there was debatable. The point to him was that he would *feel* safer. And lately he hardly ever felt safe. It was rare indeed for him to do even what he was doing now: riding on a public road, not surrounded by a force of his own men to protect him.

Only a strong motivation could make him take such a chance, and the news brought by Keefer and then clarified by Charlotte Canaday provided that kind of motivation.

Nephews! Sons of his own brother, here at Fire Creek! And he'd never even known they existed, had never even known his only brother had followed him to the United States.

And apparently, these two young men looked like him. It made the idea of meeting them all the more intriguing.

Never mind that he'd have to venture right to the jail itself—one of the domains of the enemy. He knew that Sheriff Tyler was as much in Ellison's pocket as Ellison's pocketwatch, but a man couldn't run forever. Sometimes he had to take a chance or two, just to know he was alive.

He rounded a bend, and his heart nearly jolted to a stop.

There were bodies in the road. Blood around them. One corpse lying partly atop another. He edged his horse forward a couple of steps, then, with a realization that hit with hammer force, saw that one of the corpses was that of Keefer Riley. And as he moved a little closer yet, he recognized the other as Rex Oliver, Ellison's right-hand associate, a man Patrick had secretly considered most likely to kill him.

Looking around, wondering if anyone else was

about, watching, Patrick walked up to the dead men. He could not tear his eyes away from Riley's gray, dead face. *Good God above, could the man really be dead?* He'd talked with him only a short time before, then sent him on an errand. *Go back to Fire Creek,* he'd instructed Riley. *Find out what you can about those two newcomers who reportedly look like me.*

The irony was, Riley's assignment had quickly become unnecessary. The arrival of dear Charlotte had given him the information he wanted. Now he knew who the newcomers were and why they resembled him . . . and Keefer Riley was dead because somebody had gunned him down as he faithfully undertook his assigned mission.

"I'm sorry, Keefer," Patrick whispered to his dead friend. "If I'd been a little more patient, you'd not have had to come out here at all. You'd not have been put into a position to be ambushed."

Who had killed him? And who had killed Oliver? As best Patrick could guess, the odds were the pair had killed each other. Probably Oliver had attacked Riley, Riley had defended himself, and both had come out losers.

Patrick's mind reeled. What to do now? He couldn't simply go on to Fire Creek, even to meet lost kinsmen, and leave his best friend's body in the dirt on a public road. No, he had to get Riley's body away from there, just for the sake of decency and dignity. But how?

He could drag the corpse behind his horse or perhaps tie it flopping over his horse's rump, behind the saddle.

No, no. He'd not subject Riley's body to such indignity. That would be no better than merely leaving him there. As for Oliver's corpse, it didn't matter to Patrick what became of it. Let the buzzards and dogs have it, or the ants.

Patrick made up his mind. Reluctantly, he returned to his horse, climbed into the saddle, and rode on past the dead bodies. He looked down at Riley as he passed and said, "I'll be back for you, Keefer. I'll get a wagon or something, and we'll get you taken care of. I'm sorry you died . . . especially sorry you died because you were running an errand for me."

Riley, of course, had no reply. Patrick looked away from him for the last time and continued on the road to Fire Creek.

In the front office of the local jail, Sheriff Tyler refilled the coffee cup of one of the two "preachers" in black suits, then grinned at the one named Campbell. "So you really were a preacher, were you? Before you took up your current role?"

"Just what do you believe my current role is, sheriff?" Campbell asked, grinning back.

"I think we both know," said Tyler.

"Perhaps . . . but I don't feel much comfortable talking about this openly in such a setting as this . . . and in the presence of people I do not know." Campbell shifted his eyes toward a young, slender deputy who stood in the corner of the office like a sentinel.

"Ah, yes," said the sheriff. "Sweet!" he barked at the deputy. "Go out and patrol a bit, would you?"

Harry Sweet, who had just showed up for his day's work about two minutes earlier, was the newest deputy of the sheriff's office in Fire Creek, Montana. He frowned, cleared his throat, advanced to the sheriff, leaned over, and whispered into Tyler's ear, "Sir, are you sure I should go? What if these men really are who—or what—people are saying they are? This town is full of rumors and talk. Disturbing talk. You might need help if these two decide to resist you."

"Resist me? What would I do with these men that would require resistance?"

"Why, arrest them, sir. If they really are here to kill a man, then they merit arrest . . . do they not?"

"Harry, you've got to learn to relax and trust your superior—me—about such things. If these men are who people say they are, then I know full well what to do with them."

"You do mean lock them up, I hope."

"I mean, I'll take them to see a friend of mine who will be expecting them. Mr. Bret Ellison."

Sweet's mouth dropped open. "Ellison!" he whispered, almost loudly enough for the others to hear. "But Ellison is the very man who is said to have hired killers to get Patrick Carrigan!"

"Sweet, when will you ever tell me something I don't already know?"

"I don't understand, sheriff. I mean, if Bret Ellison is trying to hire killers, that ain't legal. Not only should the killers be locked up, but Ellison should be, too."

"Sweet, get onto the street. Keep your eyes open for drunks and thieves and such. Leave bigger matters to me."

Sweet tried to grin again, but the effort faltered. "Sir, you begin to make me wonder if other things I've heard might be true."

"Things about what?"

"About you, sir . . . and Ellison. Some say he controls you."

"And some say that deputies should learn their place and when to keep their mouths closed."

"I'm sorry, sir. I didn't mean to insult you."

"I'll be insulting you and your mother and your sainted old grandmother if you don't get out of this office, leave me in peace with my guests here, and keep your thoughts to yourself from now on. You understand me, Sweet?"

"Yes, sir."

Sweet turned and left the office. He passed near the door leading back to the cell area and heard from the other side of the door a muffled call. One of the prisoners asking for a deputy. Probably wanting a cup of water or a chance to visit the outhouse. Sweet, remembering his orders, hesitated. He should get on the street as he'd been told to do. But the call from the back came again, and he muttered a mild curse and headed back to the cell block.

The call had come from the white man jailed with the black one. Sweet went to the cell and asked Rambling Jim what he needed.

"I don't need nothing," he said. "But my friend, here, Mr. Sparks, is in need of some cold water to drink."

Sweet glanced around the cell and noticed a pewter pitcher sitting in one corner. The standard kind of pitcher in which prisoners were provided water in this jail. "What's wrong with that water there?" he asked.

"It was fine . . . until I peed in it," Rambling Jim said.

"Peed in it? Why the devil did you pee in your own drinking water?"

"A man's got to pee somewhere, ain't he? And there was nobody on duty willing to take me out to the privy house. So I done what I had to do."

"I'm just grateful he didn't need to take a squat instead of just a pee," said Sparks, then flashed the quickest and faintest of smiles.

Sweet pondered, then chuckled and shuddered at the same time. He pointed at a drain in the center of the floor. "Pour that filth out of the pitcher into that hole," he said. "I'll go fetch you some clean water in a different pitcher. And no peeing in this one, right?" He glared at Rambling Jim. "And no anything else. The water will be for drinking, you understand? Just drinking."

"Just drinking," said Rambling Jim.

"I'll go fetch your water, sir," the deputy said to Sparks, whose jolted reaction caused Sweet to wonder what he'd done wrong.

"What is it?" he asked.

"I just wanted to say thank you."

"It's just water."

"Not for the water, sir. Just for calling me 'sir.'" Rambling Jim cleared his throat. "He's like me, Mr. Sparks. A progressive and fearless free-thinker."

Ain't no white man ever called me that before."

Sweet shrugged. "I just try to do right by people." He glanced up toward the front-office end of the building. "I hope others in positions of authority hold to the same practice."

He nodded a greeting at Liam and Joseph as he passed their cell and went up front on his quest for water. When he returned a few minutes later with pitcher in hand, he greeted them again, took the water around to a grateful Mickey Sparks, then returned to the Carrigan cell.

"They tell me you two are kin to Patrick Carrigan," Sweet said.

"Yes. He's our father's brother."

"Does he know you're in jail?"

"I doubt it. I doubt he knows we exist. Unless someone has told him."

"I hope nobody has," Liam threw in. "Because he might come here to find us, and if he does, I dread to think what might happen to him."

Sweet looked solemn, paused, then said, "I agree with your thinking. I have fear that our sheriff may be . . . may not be . . . I shouldn't say. Because I don't really know."

"I know what you're getting at, deputy. The sheriff, everyone says, dances on a string held in the hand of Bret Ellison, who wants our uncle dead and has hired two assassins to bring that about. The two assassins, I think, are in the front of this jail building at this moment, I believe."

"Yes. I know. And I'm afraid the sheriff has very little concern about that."

"Deputy, can you get us out of here?"

"You mean, let you go?"

"Right."

"I . . . I can't do that. I'm not authorized. It's my duty to observe the law."

Joseph stepped closer and spoke earnestly. "Is there not a higher duty to ensure that an innocent man is not murdered?"

"Yes . . . I suppose there is."

"Then ask yourself, deputy, how will you feel if you leave men locked up who will protect that innocent man, and that man in fact is killed? You let us go free, and you'll be saving a life."

"But I'm sworn to uphold the law and to follow the guidance of my superior."

"But your superior is not upholding the law but shirking it."

From the next cell, Rambling Jim said, "Men, think about it. You can't ask the deputy just to turn over his keys. He'll get himself in all kinds of trouble. But maybe, if his keys got stolen . . ." There was a muffled jangle, and the deputy turned suddenly.

"What the devil did you just do?" He slapped about his waist area, as if looking for something. "Where's my ring of keys?"

"I don't know, sir," Rambling Jim said, moving back into his cell. "Perhaps you left them up front."

Sweet's face reddened, and a vein in his forehead bulged. But he said nothing for a minute, his eyes shifting from cell to cell and his brain clearly working fast. He glared at Rambling Jim, who had his hands behind his back, and said, "Maybe I did."

The deputy wheeled and stormed up to the front of the jail, entered the front-office area, and slammed the door.

Rambling Jim pulled the ring of keys from behind his back and went to the door of his cell, where he hurriedly began trying various keys until he found one that opened the door. It creaked open; he stepped out and unlocked the Carrigan brothers' cell as well. "Good to meet you, gentlemen," he said, "and I wish you the best in keeping your uncle alive."

Rambling Jim headed for the front of the jail just as Sweet had done, boldly opened the door, and advanced out. The remaining prisoners braced to hear some sound indicating he was being stopped and returned, but none came. Either he was being allowed to walk out unmolested, or no one had noticed his departure.

"Well, Joseph? Shall we go?" Liam asked, leaving the cell.

"I suppose so . . . but I'd like to know who is up there first."

"I'll look and see," said Sparks, who still lingered for some reason.

"Be careful, then."

Sparks swept past them and to the door, which he opened slowly. Initially, he merely peered through the opening, then he stepped out and looked around.

The door remained open with Sparks in full view of the Carrigan brothers. He looked around, then faced the brothers.

"Empty!" he said. "No one is here at all!"

Liam and Joseph shared a glance. "Let's go," Liam said.

They gathered their personal possessions, including weapons and ammunition, from a cabinet up front, then were out the door together in moments, out on the street and making for the nearest alley to avoid being seen too readily.

When Charlotte Canaday found the bodies on the road, she almost fell from her horse in her hurry to dismount. She approached the bodies slowly, but not all the way, because the sight of them and the recognition of who they were sickened her so deeply she staggered to the side of the road and was sick, then found herself unable to approach them any more closely.

She shouldn't have come, wouldn't have come if she had had any anticipation of finding such a horror as this.

Yet, ironically, it was the possibility of a death on the road that had led her to make this journey to start with. When Patrick Carrigan had learned the news of his nephews' presence in Fire Creek, he'd chosen to go find them. No surprise, to Charlotte, but it made her wonder if she'd done right in telling him.

She should have realized it would make him leave the relative safety of his ranch and take to the open road, so dangerous for him of late.

If she'd anticipated finding anyone dead along the road, it would have been Patrick Carrigan, not his foreman and the foreman of the ranch owned by his greatest enemy. She'd always liked Keefer Riley, but in her heart she knew that she was grateful that it was he, and not Patrick, who had died.

She tried to figure out how this double death had happened. They must have shot each other, or some third party killed both of them.

Finding the bodies changed her plans. Though she still feared for Patrick's safety, she could not continue on as before, now that she knew what had happened to poor Riley. Reluctantly, she turned and began riding back toward the Carrigan ranch. She would give the news and let some of Patrick's men ride back out to retrieve the body of their foreman.

Sheriff Tyler was also on the road, albeit a different road on the far side of town and traveling away from Fire Creek rather than toward it. With him were the two "preachers" in black—Zeke Campbell and Charles Torval—men he now fully knew were at Fire Creek under the hire of Bret Ellison, there to find and kill Patrick Carrigan.

Ellison had forewarned Tyler of the pair's arrival

days ago. He'd not known, however, exactly how they would arrive or under what identities or circumstances. Tyler, corrupt as he was, still took no pleasure in the thought of hired killers coming to his town. He had nothing against Carrigan and no loyalty to Ellison beyond what Ellison had bought. He would not be happy when these men completed their work.

"So, how does a man get into the business of killing for hire?" he asked Torval.

"That's a hard question to answer," Torval said. "I suppose a man drifts into it, like a lawman drifting into taking money to look the other way when he needs to."

"I call it survival," Tyler said.

"That's right," said Campbell. "A man does what he has to do."

"Where does Bret Ellison live?" asked Torval.

"In an old fort—Fort Ellison, folks call it these days."

"How far?"

"Another mile and a half or thereabouts."

"I'm eager to meet this man and find out why he's so eager to get rid of this other rancher."

"Don't count on him to tell you. He seems to hold that a close secret. I don't know that answer myself."

"I expect him to tell us," Torval said. "If I'm to be expected to destroy a man, I insist on knowing why. Without that, I don't do my work."

"Nor I," said Campbell. "Nor I."

Tyler had nothing to say to that, but he did ponder that these two might find it more difficult than they expected to dictate terms to Bret Ellison. Tyler knew from experience that the man was a controlling sort and did not know the meaning of compromise or negotiation.

They rode on, until at last they topped a rise and looked down on a broad, rolling area, in the midst of which stood a neat stockade enclosing a large house and several other structures. Outside the stockade were barns and stables and outbuildings, including what looked like a large and well-built bunkhouse. Several human figures moved about on the ranch grounds.

"Gentlemen, I give you Fort Ellison," said Tyler.

"Quite impressive," said Torval.

They continued their ride, Tyler hoping they would find Ellison in a congenial mood. If he was not, the ride was probably wasted, for Ellison saw no one he did not wish to see. But given who these two men were and the fact that he had made arrangements to hire them, Tyler was optimistic that the rancher would welcome them.

They traveled down the slope until someone spotted them. Moments later, two riders moved toward them. They met outside the stockade walls, and the sheriff and the two Ellison riders talked. A minute later, the stockade door opened, and the entire group rode inside.

CHAPTER TEN

The long-sought meeting with their uncle came in a most unexpected manner for Joseph and Liam Carrigan. But it proved every bit as gratifying as they ever had hoped.

After their break from the jail, they moved through alleys and empty lots to the other side of town, hats pulled low and eyes averted from most they passed in order to avoid being readily identified. Their resemblance to their uncle was like a brand on them in this town.

They reached the edge of town, then realized they had no idea where to go. They wanted more than anything to find the residence of their uncle, but so far no one had told them where it was.

Then a stroke of luck. Down a side street, they saw a familiar figure, keeping to the shadows. Rambling Jim Murphy, looking conspicuous in his obvious attempt to be inconspicuous, did not initially notice the three men until they moved into the alley where he was, and their forms blocked the light and cast shadows. He turned, startled, then looked relieved when he recognized them.

"So you made it out without getting caught, did you?"

"We did. But now we need your help, Jim," Liam said.

"What kind of help?"

"We have to know where to find the Carrigan ranch. You can take us there?"

"I can, but I don't want to run across no deputies or sheriffs in the process."

"Nor do we."

"Well, I'll take you there. But if somebody comes after us, it's every man for himself."

Liam turned to Sparks. "What about you, Mickey? You coming, too?"

Sparks shrugged. "No reason to, I don't suppose. Maybe no reason to stay around this town at all. It's brought me little but trouble so far."

"You need work, Mickey?" Joseph asked. "Maybe you could find it with our uncle. We'll be asking for work ourselves."

"I could use work, but I don't know whether I want to work in the midst of a range war. Could be dangerous."

"It could be," admitted Joseph.

"Think I'll hold off on asking for work just now."

"Well, that's your choice to make. You want to go with us just for the ride?"

"No . . . I suppose I'll just move on to the next place."

"Where is that?"

"I'm not sure. I've got a job I need to do. An old job that's been undone for too long."

"So you do have work."

"I've got something to do . . . I'll say no more than that."

"You know, we're going to have to go to the livery and get our horses," said Joseph.

"Let's head that way."

"I been pleased to meet you men," Sparks said.

"It's been a pleasure to meet you, too," Joseph said.

"You men be careful, especially once you find your uncle. He's in danger, then you're in danger, too."

"I know."

Liam put a hand on Sparks's shoulder. "Come with us, Mickey. Maybe we'll find things aren't as bad as you're saying."

Sparks relaxed. "Well . . . maybe I'll come along after all."

"Good," Liam said.

"That's right," said Joseph. "Glad to have you come along."

They shook hands and headed as a group toward the livery.

Leonard was surprised to see the group that appeared at the livery, believing them all to be still in the jail. Sensing the trustworthiness of the young man, they admitted to him that they were away from the jail illegitimately and asked him to keep their escape a secret. If the law came asking whether they had come to claim their horses, he was to admit they had but say they had forced him to turn the horses over so he could keep himself out of trouble.

When they were saddled up and ready to leave and Leonard was paid and well tipped for his service, Leonard walked to the stable doors and swung one of them open.

"Gentlemen, it appears that the way is clear if you want to go."

They mounted and rode to the door, Liam in the lead, ready to go out first. But Leonard suddenly moved in front of him, blocking his way, and stared at something outside. "Wait!" he said quietly. "Not yet."

Liam looked out to see what had the boy's attention and saw a rider coming up the street in their direction. He was some distance away as yet, and no features were clear, but there was something in his build and posture that seemed familiar to Liam. And the closer he drew, the more Liam was frozen with a sense of awe . . . but a familiar sense. He'd felt this same thing before, and not long ago.

It came to him after a moment. This was the same thing he'd felt when he looked up during Professor Marvel's ghost show and saw the image of what appeared to be his father in that column of smoke on the stage.

But this was different. No phantom, not a projection of some actor or photographic image. This was a real man, riding slowly down the street and beginning to draw notice from some nearby. Liam watched as a man on a boardwalk stepped to the street and tipped his hat at the rider, who nodded at him in a friendly manner. A woman crossed the street to speak to the rider as well. The rider removed his hat while talking with her, and Liam got his first good look at the man's face.

Dear God, it was his own father! Older now, and back from the dead . . . living and breathing in the world again.

Joseph moved his horse up beside Liam's and looked out. Liam heard his brother suck in his breath sharply.

"Liam, it's him. It's him!"

"I know . . . it's Pa, our father."

"Can't be him, Liam. He's dead. It's Patrick Carrigan."

"You're right, sir," said Leonard. "And it's rare

indeed to see that man come into town these days. It's just too dangerous for him to do it often."

Patrick Carrigan put his hat back on and rode past the woman who had been talking to him. He headed straight toward the livery door but halted abruptly when he saw the pair looking back at him from the doorway. Though his face was now shadowed again by the brim of his hat, Liam could see enough of his features to comprehend that Patrick was as surprised to see their faces as they were to see his. That family similarity of appearance again.

For more than a minute, without words, the two Carrigan brothers stared at the uncle they had crossed the country to find, and he stared back at them.

Then Liam reached up, took off his hat, and smiled at his uncle. Patrick Carrigan smiled in turn and began riding again, his horse slowly plodding toward them.

CHAPTER ELEVEN

Patrick Carrigan dismounted and walked slowly toward the two younger men who sat astride their horses in the doorway of the Fire Creek livery stable. There were others inside the stable, farther in, but Patrick gave them little heed. He could not take his eyes off the two just inside the door, especially the taller one.

Leading his horse, Patrick walked up to that taller one and looked up at him. He could not keep a tear from pooling in his eye. "You are the very image of your father," he said. "When I first saw you, I thought I was looking into the past, looking at him."

Liam grinned. "I thought the same when I saw you, Uncle Patrick. You look just like Pa. Only a little more gray than he was."

"I've got a few years on him," Patrick said, grinning back. "Is he . . . gone? The letter I received from my son said that my brother had died."

Liam lost his smile and gained some tears. Normally, he was embarrassed to show much emotion, but in these circumstances it didn't seem to matter. "Yes, he's gone. Some years now. He came to this country looking for you, Uncle Patrick. May I call you that . . . Uncle Patrick?"

"You may. You are . . ."

"I'm Liam. This here is Joseph." Joseph, smiling, leaned over and extended his hand to his uncle.

"Men, I'm pleased to have found you," Patrick said. "Good Irishmen, the both of you, like your father. I rode to town today to look for you. Miss Charlotte Canaday informed me you were here and told me who you were. I was not prepared for such unexpected news."

"It's truly a joy to meet you at last," Joseph said. "I've believed for a long time now that it was God's destiny that we should find you, and we've come a long way to do it. And we met your son, Pat, along the way. And I take it that Miss Canaday gave his letter to you, as we asked her to."

"She did. I've read it through and appreciate having it. I'll be keeping it forever, like a treasure. Did you read it yourselves?"

"No, sir. The letter was not for us, and we did not read it. But we did spend some time with Patrick and know some of what he probably told you. His situation is good. He's found himself a good woman to spend his life with."

"That's good, yes . . . but I wish that woman had been Charlotte," said Patrick. "I've never known a finer young lady. If I were younger myself, I'd be inclined to try to make her my own."

"She does seem a true gem," Liam said. "And I'm a good judge of women. Women and I get on very well."

"That's true," said Joseph. "But the kind of women Liam usually gets on with are not the marrying sort, generally. More the sporting variety."

"I've known more than a few of that sort myself," said Patrick. "Liam, I expect you and I might have more similarities than mere facial appearance."

"Could be!" Liam said.

Patrick, relaxing now that the moment of meeting was past, slumped back in his saddle a little. "You know, boys—and I know you're far from boys, but you're boys to an old man like me—I've been looking for the arrival of two newcomers to Fire Creek. Just not kinfolk kind of newcomers."

Joseph nodded solemnly. "We know about that, sir, and it's our sad duty to tell you that those other newcomers are also in town. Two men, in black suits, claiming to be preachers. But preachers they aren't."

"You know much about my current situation in this place? And a man named Ellison?"

"We've heard some things."

"We've heard that it's so bad folks call it a war."

"The Fire Creek war . . . that's right." Patrick

chuckled abruptly. "A lot of times, these range wars start over such things as water and grazing rights, or fence-stringing sodbusters, and so on. But not this one. This one is pure personal. And one-sided. I'd be glad to live in peace with Ellison if he'd have it. But Bret ain't that way. Never has been."

"You talk as if you've known him a long time."

"And so I have. Years and years. I knew him when my hair and his both was dark and thick as the night."

"Have you talked to him, tried to make peace?"

"I've tried. Haven't succeeded. And I've got to be careful these days even about showing myself. Ellison has eyes and ears everywhere . . . and hands willing to do dirty work for him. Including pulling triggers." Patrick paused and looked around, made nervous by his own words. "Let's move inside the livery a little further."

They did as he asked, and while they moved, Patrick nodded greeting at the others there. He spoke to young Leonard, who nodded respectfully, then looked over at Rambling Jim. "Hello, Jim," he said. "How you faring?"

"Can't complain," Jim replied. "Is that shed I built you still standing?"

"Hell, no," said Patrick. "Old Skillet set it afire, smoking a cigar inside it. Went in there one afternoon to sneak a nap, lit up a cigar, and got the place to blazing like one of his cookstove fires. The old varmint barely got his hind end out of there before the place fell down all aflame. It was a spectacle to see, Rambling Jim. But too bad as well . . . it was a good shed, even if it was a tinderbox."

"Build you another one if you want. I'm looking for work. I'll sweep your floors, clean your barn stalls, polish your boots for Sunday meeting. Whatever you want done, I'll do . . . if you'll pay me."

"I don't need no boot polishing, but if you want to rebuild that shed, same terms as before, consider yourself hired."

"Thank you. But I got to be honest with you, I've worked for Ellison since I worked for you."

"What of it? His money spends as well as mine. And he's got more of it to pay out."

"Well, just given the way things is hereabouts these days, I thought I should tell you I'd worked for him, just so you'd know. In case it put a bad taste in your mouth regarding me."

"Only bad tastes I get, I get from eating Skillet's son-of-a-bitch stew," Patrick said. "You're hired, Rambling Jim. Unless you've got ties and obligations to Ellison you're not telling me about."

"Not a one. I'm obliged for the work. Now, let me ask you about my good negro friend here. This is Mickey Sparks, and he's in need of work, too. Can he work with me on the shed and whatever else you might need done?" Jim turned to Mickey. "You can swing a hammer, can't you?"

Patrick looked closely at Mickey, his eyes narrowing. "Mickey Sparks . . . is that your name?"

"Yes, sir, it is."

"Have I met you somewhere before, Mickey Sparks?"

"Where would that have been, sir?"

"I don't know, but I swear, boy . . . I mean, I swear, Sparks, I think I know you. I know I've seen your face before. You sure the name is Sparks?"

"A man knows his own name, doesn't he? And maybe you have seen me before. Sometimes the world is small, sir. Maybe we have met. Sometime past."

"Philosophical fellow, this one," Patrick said to Liam. "'Sometimes the world is small.' Did you hear him say that?"

"With my own ears."

"You seem a smart man, Sparks. Are you an educated man of color?"

"I think I am smart enough, sir. But I'm not educated, not school-educated, anyway. I just know a lot of things I've learned along the way. That the world is small . . . and that a man can't run from his past deeds. They come back eventually, and the balances settle. It's wrote into the way the world is made. A balance that's knocked off center tries its best to right itself. It's just the way things is."

Liam, listening, thought, *There he goes again. More of that "balance" talk of his. What does Sparks mean by all that?*

Patrick grunted in reply to Sparks but said nothing. He looked at Sparks with narrowed eyes, keeping his thoughts unspoken, then returned attention to his nephews.

"I regret that you have to find me at such a difficult time and place," he said.

"How bad is this war, really?" Liam asked.

"Worse than it was," said Patrick. "On the way to town, I found the bodies of two men dead in the road. One is my foreman, Keefer Riley, the other the foreman of Bret Ellison, a foul kind of man named Rex Oliver. To all appearance, the pair of them shot at each other at the same time . . . and both shots were good."

"Damn!" Liam exclaimed.

"We had an encounter with Keefer Riley ourselves," said Joseph. "He was at the ghost show in town and saw us there, and later he looked at us through the window of the café. He was identified to us by someone who knows him, so I'm certain it was Keefer Riley. And now he's dead?"

"He's very dead," said Patrick. "And it's tragic. Riley had his flaws, and he could be blind to anything that was not how he desired to perceive it, but at heart he was a fine and good man, and there has never been another man more loyal as a friend and employee. He would do anything to ensure my safety and, in fact, this very night came to my house to tell me about two strangers in town, men who happened to resemble me greatly . . . men he'd seen at the ghost show."

"Us, you mean," said Liam.

"Obviously so. He didn't know who you were, of course, but when Charlotte came in with Pat's letter, I was able to surmise your identities by putting together what the letter said with what Keefer told me."

"I'm sorry he was killed," Joseph said. "It's terrible indeed that this war has gone beyond a feud between two men and is now something embroiling others."

"I never intended that my problems with Bret Ellison should bring danger to my employees," Patrick said. "And perhaps each of you should consider that thoroughly before you associate yourself with me too closely."

"We're already associated, by blood and heritage," Liam said. "I've got no hesitation."

"And I need a job," said Rambling Jim.

"I suppose I'm in that same boat," said Sparks in a lower tone.

"Come with me, gentlemen," said Patrick. "Let's ride together to my ranch, where it will be my pleasure to host you for a dinner of excellent beef this very evening."

"Best offer I've had in a year," said Liam. "Uncle, we accept."

"Then let's ride."

They heard the battle well before they reached its site. It puzzled most of the group, but Patrick Carrigan had a dreadful suspicion the moment he heard the first burst of shots. He sped his horse a little, then changed his mind and slowed. What was going on ahead was probably nothing a man would want to speed into . . . particularly Patrick Carrigan.

"What do you think, Patrick?" asked Joseph.

"I have a suspicion that some of my men and some of Ellison's may be facing off up ahead. It sounds like that fight is going on near where the bodies lay."

"Then let's approach the scene carefully," suggested Joseph. "And you, Uncle Patrick, you should remain out of sight."

"I can't live in a hole, my friends. And if my men are in trouble up there, I'll sure not balk from giving them all the same help they'd give me."

"I'm going up," Liam said. "I want to see what's going on here."

Before anyone could suggest otherwise, Liam spurred his horse to a near run and made his way with all haste toward whatever battle was going on ahead.

* * *

In future histories of the Fire Creek area, the altercation Liam and the others ran across would be recorded as the one true battle of the War of Fire Creek. Until it broke out, violence had been somewhat isolated and limited, occasional shots fired at lone cowboys out on the range or small groups of cowboys exchanging usually harmless shots.

But the deaths of the two ranch foremen on a public road and their discovery by representatives of their various ranches led to something much bigger than a mere mostly symbolic exchange of overshot bullets.

When Liam reached the fight, he saw that providence had been on his side in at least one way: the Carrigan group chanced to come onto the scene on the side of the road held by the Carrigan men already engaged in battle. Within moments, he was among the fighters, taking cover in roadside brush and sending shots toward a similarly situated group from the Ellison ranch.

The fight was noisy, intense, but so far not very bloody. A few men were nipped by bullets, and one man on the Ellison side went down unconscious with a bloody furrow on the side of his head. Joseph joined the fight at Liam's side and grunted almost as quickly as he got into position when a bullet cut through the fleshy part of his forearm.

He withdrew to receive a quick, makeshift bandaging, then returned to the fight, wounding two Ellison men in short order.

The Battle of Fire Creek Road went on for nearly an hour and ended with no victory for either side. The battle dissolved more than ended, fighters growing weary and unwilling to continue. This happened most notably on the Ellison side, and the Carrigan brothers took note of it.

Perhaps the will to take risks and do battle was not nearly so great among Ellison's men as it was on Ellison's part himself, Joseph noted to Liam.

"What do you expect?" Liam replied. "This isn't really their war. These men here are fighting at the moment in retaliation for two dead foremen, and that anger won't hold force for long."

Liam was right. A little more than an hour after the Carrigan brothers and their group chanced upon it, the Battle of Fire Creek Road was over. The Carrigan band, now enlarged, returned to their saddles, gathered up the wounded and the dead body of Keefer Riley, and headed on toward the Carrigan ranch.

Joseph tugged a little at the fresh bandage around his left forearm and winced slightly.

"Too tight?" asked Allie.

"No . . . just hurts a little."

"Kind of you to come here and help Mr. Carrigan," the maid observed, smiling prettily at Joseph.

He couldn't help but smile back at such a beautiful face. "Well, he is our uncle, after all. And family should help family."

She nodded. "I agree with that. I wish I had family myself."

"You're alone in the world?"

"Yes. My mother was the last to go. She died two years ago. She was a maid here before I was. Mr. Carrigan let me take her place in the household."

"Very good of him."

"Yes."

The girl, though uneducated and of simple raising, struck Joseph's intuition as someone with sense about her. He decided to ask her a question that had been on his mind since the fight that had wounded him and Liam, who had already been bandaged and now reclined on a sofa in the main room, sipping a glass of wine provided by his uncle.

"Allie, do you know Bret Ellison?"

"I have met him. I have delivered messages to his man, the local sheriff."

"Yes indeed, his man."

"I don't know him well."

"Let me ask this: Has anyone ever tried to simply sit down and talk to him about his dispute with Patrick? A kind of peace emissary, I mean. Has anyone ever even tried to do that?"

"Not to my knowledge, no. I don't think Mr. Patrick

would allow any of his people to try such a thing. It would be like Daniel walking into the den of lions for anyone associated with him to walk into Fort Ellison."

"But if you'll remember the story, Allie, the lions did not devour Daniel. And maybe such a visit would generate good and peaceful results rather than violent ones."

"You might be right, sir."

"After what happened today, men shooting at one another, people being hurt and maybe killed, surely both Patrick and Ellison would be eager to see some sort of peace made. They can't possibly want this to continue."

"I don't know about that, sir. I think Mr. Patrick would make peace, but Ellison is a hard and mean man. He holds some deep old grudge."

"Do you know what it is?"

"I have heard it rumored that he holds Mr. Patrick responsible for the death of his wife. I don't know that this is truly what he believes, but I have been told that."

"I have a plan, Allie. I'm going to try something no one has tried before. I'm going to find Bret Ellison and talk to him about ending this absurd conflict. I'm going to be Daniel and walk into the den of lions. I'm going to attempt a bit of diplomacy with Bret Ellison. I don't think anyone has done that yet. Do you know what I mean when I say 'diplomacy'?"

"Yes, sir. You really intend to do that, sir?"

"I do."

"It would be very dangerous. Mr. Patrick wouldn't want you to do it. He's said for a long time that words will never stop Ellison. He says Ellison is too determined to see him destroyed, and nothing less will suit him."

"Someone has to try something. There were people shot out there today, all because of some conflict between two stubborn men, a conflict they won't even explain. The explanation you gave is the most specific information I've been able to obtain so far."

"I don't know that my information is right, sir."

"But perhaps it is. The death of a wife could generate the kind of depth of feeling that seems to be driving Ellison. It would make sense."

"I don't think you should meet with Ellison alone, sir. It will not be safe."

"Promise me you'll tell no one what I'm doing, Allie. I have to try this."

She was reluctant but, with prompting, agreed to keep his secret. "But do you know even where to find Fort Ellison?" she asked him.

"I don't. Can you tell me?"

"If you will promise me you will return alive, I'll draw you a little map to get you there."

"I'll return alive, Allie. I have no wish to leave this world just yet."

She smiled feebly and went to a nearby desk for

pencil and paper. She worked a few minutes, then went over the map with Joseph and gave it to him. "This is excellent," he said. "I'll find it without difficulty."

He patted her hand, took the map, and left the room. Allie stood and looked in the direction he'd gone, a worried expression on her face. Then she gathered up her bandaging supplies and left the room herself.

On a sofa that faced a large fireplace at the front of the room, a figure sat up slowly and peered over the back of the sofa. Mickey Sparks had been there all along, unseen by either Joseph or Allie. He'd heard the entire conversation.

Indecision showed in his face. He stood and paced a few moments before the fireplace, thinking hard. Muttering something to himself, he turned and headed out of the room suddenly. Minutes later, he was out of the house and at the stable, saddling his horse in preparation for a long ride to Fort Ellison on the heels of Joseph Carrigan.

Fearing that word of the battle on the road had reached the ears of the sheriff, Joseph did not travel through town but around it, circling Fire Creek to reach on its far side the road that led toward Fort Ellison. Once past the town, he felt less worried about Tyler and his deputies but more conscious of moving ever deeper into Ellison territory. And as he advanced, pausing twice to consult his map by matchlight, he began to wonder just how he was going to manage the task he'd set for himself and just what he would find to say to Bret Ellison. He was, after all, not assigned by Patrick to deliver any message on his behalf and therefore could not really speak for his uncle. Still, he felt intuitively that he was doing the right thing. He was at least making an attempt to be a peacemaker.

And Ellison would not know that this was purely one man's unauthorized attempt. Ellison would perceive this as something authorized by Patrick Carrigan. His responsiveness to that perception would tell Joseph much about the chances for finding a peaceful way to end the Fire Creek war.

Joseph saw the stockade at last and was struck by its size. A good deal larger than he'd anticipated. It still looked like a military installation except for the outbuildings and barns and so on around it. Joseph halted his horse in a dark place where he could not be seen and studied the scene for a long time. How could he safely get into the fort? How could he contact Ellison? Would Ellison even be willing to talk to him?

Then a darker thought: What if Ellison made him a prisoner, a pawn to use in his game with Patrick Carrigan? The possibility of being taken hostage had crossed Joseph's mind before, but only now did the full force of that possibility strike him.

It was almost enough to change his mind and send him back toward the Carrigan ranch. He turned and looked over his shoulder, seriously thinking of riding back the way he'd come. As he looked, he noticed something moving out in the darkness, as if someone was behind him.

An Ellison man? A patroling sentry? Just some local out for a nighttime ride? Or had someone followed him from the Carrigan ranch?

"Liam?" Joseph whispered. "Is that you, Liam?"

No one replied, and he did not see any further motion. Perhaps he'd simply imagined it.

Saying a prayer that he would be kept safe and find his peace mission productive, Joseph rode out into the open again and began his descent toward the closed doors of the Fort Ellison stockade.

Mickey Sparks cursed softly at himself. He'd grown too careless, gotten too close. He'd not intended for Joseph Carrigan to detect that he'd been followed. At least Joseph didn't know who his follower was. He'd whispered the name of his brother, not Mickey.

Sparks watched as Joseph became a smaller, more distant figure, hard to see against the darkness of Fort Ellison's strong wall. How did the man plan to get inside? And what would he do?

Sparks wondered if this was an assassination mission, Joseph Carrigan going out alone to eliminate the enemy right in his own quarters. It might be. But it seemed to Sparks that a mission like that seemed more likely for Liam Carrigan than for Joseph. The two were similar in many ways but quite different in temperament.

Sparks moved his horse behind a tree when he saw a little band of riders come around the side of the stockade, circling toward Joseph. Sparks's heart raced—they'd spotted Joseph. Probably some sentry along that wall, hidden from easy view. Any man who felt the need to live inside a stockade probably kept sentinels posted.

Barely breathing, Sparks watched and waited for the sound of gunfire. They'd gun Joseph down, surely. Or Joseph would try to shoot his way out and make a run for it.

But neither thing happened. The riders reached Joseph without any violence breaking out and circled him. Sparks saw Joseph hand over his weapons and speak to one of the riders. Then the entire group moved toward the big stockade doors, which slowly opened a short distance and admitted them. Then the doors closed again, and Sparks drew in a slow breath.

Joseph Carrigan was inside Fort Ellison. What would happen now Sparks could not guess. But he had to find a way to get inside himself. Without an escort such as Joseph had. Without being seen at all.

CHAPTER TWELVE

Allie knocked on the door of Patrick Carrigan's bedroom and again glanced up and down the hallway, hoping no one saw her there. Some of those around the Carrigan ranch were gossips who lived to find an opportunity to injure the reputations of others. For her to be seen knocking on the door of her employer at this hour would not be good.

"Who is it?" Patrick asked, his voice sounding sleepy.

"It's me, sir—Allie. I must tell you something."

"Allie? Why here? Why at this hour?"

"It's quite important, sir. I promised I wouldn't tell, but I have to do so, or else Mr. Joseph might find himself in great trouble."

"Joseph?" She heard him rise, heard him putting on trousers and coming toward the door. She stepped back as he opened it.

Patrick was just putting on his shirt again. He stared at her, then said, "Well, tell me."

"I promised Mr. Joseph I would not tell, but I fear for him if I don't. He left here, sir, to go to Fort Ellison and talk in person to Bret Ellison. He believes that maybe he can make peace if he can persuade him to do so. He believes he can talk an end to all the trouble."

"Good God!" Patrick exclaimed. "He actually went there tonight?"

"Yes, sir."

"How long ago?"

"Long enough to be there by now, sir."

"You waited that long to tell me?"

"I'd promised him, sir. I didn't know the right thing to do."

"You've done right in telling me. You should have told me sooner, though."

"I'm sorry."

"I've got to go after him."

"What, sir?"

"I can't let him take that kind of risk for me and not respond. I've got to go to Fort Ellison myself . . . right away."

"They'll . . . they'll try to kill you, sir."

"Maybe not. Maybe I'll surprise them so much they won't do that. And even if they do, better me than Joseph. This is my war, not his. And not that of the men who were shot today. This never should have gone so far, and it's my fault for not stopping it."

"I wish I had come sooner. Maybe you could have stopped him before he got there."

"You never know, Allie. Maybe this is as it should be. Maybe it's been my duty all along to go confront Bret face to face, man to man."

"You'll not go alone, sir, will you?"

"No," said a voice from down the hall, startling both her and Patrick. Liam Carrigan stepped from around the corner of the hallway. "I'll be going with him. It's my brother, after all. Sorry, Patrick. I wasn't trying to eavesdrop. I was just in my room and heard your voice when I stepped out into the hall. I heard it all."

"Liam, I insist you stay here. I'll not see a second nephew endangered over something I should have found a way to end long ago."

"It would be suicide for you to go alone. And that would leave both you and Joseph in danger. If they kill you, they'll kill him, too, just to make sure he never told about it."

"And you think that by coming, you alter the odds enough to make a difference?"

"Maybe not, but I'm obliged to go. This is family, and you don't leave family in a bad situation. It's what my father taught me, Uncle Patrick."

Patrick could not counter those words. He nodded slowly. "Come well armed, Liam. I'll do the same."

"I will be. I'll see you at the stable, Uncle Patrick."

"Be careful, sirs," said Allie. "If something happens to you because of this, I'll feel responsible, because I'm the one who told."

"Keep the blame where it belongs. On Bret Ellison. And me."

"Her name was Ann," Bret Ellison said, looking up at the portrait above the fireplace. Joseph sat nearby in a comfortable chair, now unguarded except by Ellison himself, who kept a pistol within quick reach on a table beside his chair but away from Joseph. The guards who had brought Joseph in had been sent out; what Ellison was saying was intended for no ears but Joseph's.

"Patrick and I were friends when I first met her. It was in Missouri. Patrick had come there from New York. He'd first settled in New York when he came over from Ireland, you see, but he didn't take to city life. It was particularly hard for Irishmen in the city. They weren't well received by many. So he looked west and ended up in Missouri, where I met him while he was working as a clerk in a feed and hardware store. I'd just entered the livestock business—my family has always had money from the shipping and trade operations my grandfather was involved in—and I got to know Patrick despite our very different means and circumstances. We became good friends, just two young men, reckless and looking for fortune and pleasure. And we both had less than our share of good sense in how we went about that."

"Where did you meet Ann?"

"Her father was a local granger and livestock dealer—quite well-off, really, his wealth mostly in good Missouri farm and range land. She was talking to Patrick in the store the first time I saw her. I could tell by how she looked at him that he had gained her strong interest—and it made me jealous, I admit. I vowed to myself that I'd gain that young woman as my own and get her heart away from handsome Patrick Carrigan.

"And I did. With effort, for she cared much about him, and he could be a charming fellow when he wanted to be. But when I determine to do something, my friend, I don't stop until it's done. So in the end, I became her beau, her lover, the man she told her friends she wanted to marry. Eventually, we did marry. It was the best thing that ever happened to me, before or since.

"But it hurt Patrick. Filled him with jealousy. That's why he killed her, I believe. Jealousy."

"Wait . . . Patrick *killed* her? Good Lord!"

"Yes. He did kill her."

"I can't believe . . . how could he just . . . surely he didn't do such a thing! What were the circumstances of the killing?"

Ellison pulled a cigar from a box on the table, clipped its end, and lit it slowly. He offered one to Joseph, who was tempted but under the circumstances decided not to accept even small gifts from such a one as Ellison.

"The circumstances, you ask. Ah, yes. Hoping for some explanation that will not require you to see your uncle for what he is and what he really did. Sorry, sir, but I cannot help you. What I have to tell you can only further lower your perception of Patrick Carrigan's character. And I'm afraid I must also confess to an old sin of my own." He puffed the cigar again, shifted position, and cleared his throat. "I told you that Patrick and I were young men and not the most sensible. We did a foolish thing together, a wrong thing, one I've not confessed to anyone before. We committed a robbery, Patrick and I. A small bank, in a small town along the big river. Why we did it, I don't know. Impulse . . . recklessness . . . the sense of invulnerability common to foolish young men. In any case, we did this crime, and successfully. We got away with the money, which was to be divided evenly between us. But Patrick betrayed me. He took my share of the money for himself, hid it away. But Ann found out where he had placed it and tried to get it for me. I wish she hadn't, but she did. Patrick caught her . . . and shot her. He claimed he did it because she was stealing from him, but I think he killed her mostly because she chose me above him."

Ellison paused, and tears came to his eyes. "Not a day passes when I do not relive that terrible day, the day Patrick took from me the only truly valuable thing in my life. I can never do anything but hate him for that. I stand beneath Ann's portrait and weep like a child, Mr. Carrigan, I won't deny that. I weep because I loved her so much and lost her, and I weep because I ever embroiled myself with your uncle, a man who proved more wicked than I could imagine, wicked enough to murder a beautiful, dear, perfect young woman who loved her life and loved me as well."

"I don't know what to say to that," Joseph said.

"Can you understand now why I cannot simply exist side by side with Patrick Carrigan? Why I cannot simply say, 'Everything's all right, Patrick, let's just you and me be friends and get along'? I cannot forgive what he did—for my own sake and mostly for Ann's."

"How did you and Patrick end up in the Montana Territory?" asked Joseph.

"Chance . . . or maybe some kind of destiny, either divine or diabolical. After Ann died, I wanted to pursue the arrest and prosecution of Patrick Carrigan, but how could I do that when at the heart of the crime was a bank robbery in which I was a participant? So the matter hung fire until eventually the robbery was forgotten and dismissed as unsolved. I tried my best to make some peace with the idea of living in a world that did not include Ann but did include Patrick Carrigan. But I couldn't do it. Eventually, I turned my life interests elsewhere, wound up in Kansas, then Texas, and finally came here. With some effort, I was able to obtain this abandoned military fort and convert it into my base of operations. My cattle thrived, and my success and wealth multiplied. And then, abruptly, when at last I began to feel free of the past, another rancher came on the scene."

"Patrick."

"Who else? It was like waking from a nightmare to find that the nightmare suddenly was real. The first time I laid eyes on him here in the territory and knew that life had thrown us back together again, I thought my heart would stop. The hatred that rose in me was as hot as flame . . . and it only grew as time passed. Patrick made seeming attempts to rebuild some sort of friendship between us, and I actually tried to go along with that for a time. But it could not be, not with what he'd done to *her.*" Ellison's eyes turned briefly toward the portrait above the mantel. "It was not long before I knew there was nothing for me to do but to destroy him. She is worthy of being avenged. And I will destroy him. If it destroys me as well, if it takes me to the gallows, I'll still destroy him. I owe it to her."

"And what would be different if Patrick were dead? You would still not have Ann back with you."

"No, but her soul would rest more peacefully, as would mine, to know that she was avenged. I believe it is my proper role to be her avenger, and I believe it is my destiny to succeed in achieving it. Do you believe in destiny, Mr. Carrigan?"

Joseph stared into the fireplace. "I do, sir. I believe, in fact, that it was my destiny, and Liam's, to come here and find our uncle. The way it all happened was too unlikely for it to have been mere chance. I believe we were literally sent here." He paused and looked at Ellison. "And surely we were not sent here simply to sit by and allow him to be destroyed for the sake of some old sin."

Ellison waved his hand toward the portrait of his beloved. "We are not talking here about an old sin, my friend, but about a person robbed of her very life, a life cut short for no good reason, a murder of the most cruel and horrendous nature. Every day that passes in this world with her not a part of it extends and lengthens that sin, brings it from the past to the present."

"Mr. Ellison, let me simply say this as straightforwardly as I can: Whatever happened in the past, no matter how unjust it was or how much suffering it caused, no matter how it ruins your present life, nothing will be gained by a second murder. Patrick's death would change nothing. And if there is anything my brother and I can do to protect him, we will. We owe that to him as his kinsmen. His own son is not here, but we will act in his stead to protect Patrick Carrigan as best we can."

Ellison smiled coldly. "I'll speak just as forthrightly to you as you have to me: There is nothing you or your brother can do to halt any intention I have regarding your uncle's fate. I am a man of power and determination, sir, and once I make my determination, I carry it out. I have been merciful so far. Had I truly put my effort to it, he would be dead already. But here, today, I reach a turning point and declare that Patrick Carrigan will not be allowed to go through his life with the evil he did to my dear wife left unpunished. It simply cannot be allowed to stand."

Joseph's throat tightened; he could not immediately find his voice. But his mind screamed at him that he had been a fool even to make this effort. Clearly, it would not be possible to end this absurd conflict with mere words. And in fact, he might have made things worse by coming there. Ellison was not open to persuasion. His course was set and would not be changed by anything Joseph would say.

"Then you and I, sir, are inescapably on opposing courses," Joseph said.

"Why, of course we are, if you remain stubbornly determined to protect the vermin that is your uncle.

Did you think I could be persuaded to change? It cannot happen. Not now, not ever. I'll never draw a truly peaceful breath until I have rid the world—*my world*—of Patrick Carrigan, the murderer of my dear, forever lost Ann."

Holding his breath and praying he would make no noise, Mickey Sparks hefted his muscular form to the top of the stockade and held himself there while he made a quick scan of the enclosure. If there were sentinels inside, he did not see them. He could not hold his current position much longer, so he decided to take his chances. Pushing up a little higher, he carefully shifted his weight, then pushed off at just the right moment and dropped inside.

The drop seemed much easier than the climb had been, but it also seemed much farther. He hit hard but on his feet. Being slightly flat-footed, Sparks suffered upon impact, his arches shooting pain up his calves, but with a few twists of his ankle, he set things right again, and the pain went away. He moved toward the nearest shed, being potentially exposed to view where he was.

Hiding in the darkness behind the shed, he checked his pistol, which remained firmly strapped into his holster. A second and much smaller hide-out pistol was tucked in a shoulder holster under his jacket. It, too, was safely in place. He quickly checked the loading of both weapons, then began trying to formulate a further plan.

Where was Joseph Carrigan? How could he find him without betraying his own presence?

He cautiously stepped out into the open and headed toward a different building, a tack shed with the door slightly ajar. But no one was inside, he was glad to find, and he ducked in and felt much better hidden than before.

And from there, out the window, he could see Ellison's house much more clearly. There were several lighted windows. He wondered which window Ellison was behind and if Joseph was in there, too. Probably so; he'd come to talk to Ellison, after all. Sparks examined the house more closely, hoping he'd chance to see something informative. His eyes scanned from window to window, then something outside the house drew his attention.

Two men were looking in his direction, concentrating hard on the shed in which he hid. Could they actually see him through the window? Hard to believe they could, as dark as it was inside the structure. He crouched low, minimizing himself, just in case, and watched them. They did not move from where they were, but he had a strong impression that they were watching something he could not see, not merely staring at a dark tack shed.

Sparks looked around the shed, hopeful of finding

a back way out in case those two watchers, or others, began to advance toward his hiding place. But there was no second exit. Glowering, he moved back toward the door, glancing out the window and noticing that the pair no longer were visible. During the time he'd searched the shed, they'd left their place near Ellison's house and had gone Sparks knew not where.

Touching his pistol to reassure himself, he positioned himself at the door, ready to open it and slip out. He was going to have to go to Ellison's house, and into it, to achieve anything. Perhaps now was the time to make the move, while there was no one in obvious sight of him. He took another step closer to the door of the shed and reached up to push it open.

The door exploded outward before he could touch it, and a dark figure filled the doorway. Stunned by surprise, Sparks froze as the figure burst inside and a hard fist hammered his jaw, knocking him down.

Sparks's head slammed against a support post, rendering him half senseless for a few moments. As he lay there on his side, he saw a second figure come through the door and kneel beside him.

"Who's this darky?" the newcomer asked.

"I don't know . . . ain't sure I've seen him before."

"You know, I think I did see him . . . today, out in the fight along the road. He was one of Carrigan's men."

"Hell, we ought to shoot him right here," said the other. "I got no use for a Carrigan man, and particular less for one who's a darky besides." The man leaned over and looked down into Sparks's face. "I don't like your kind, boy. I won't lie to you about that. I despise your breed. You hear me, boy?"

Mickey, gradually regaining his mental clarity and losing the ringing in his ears, reached subtly to his side and slipped out a knife sheathed near his pistol. He wrapped his hand around the grip. The man who had just spoken to him stood and backed away, the other man, already standing, stepping back as well.

Letting his head clear a moment more, Sparks drew in two deep breaths and flexed his leg muscles, preparing for his next move. At that point, one of the pair, the one who had leaned over him and insulted him, drew back a booted foot and kicked Mickey in the side. He felt a rib bend and almost snap, and he twisted in pain, light exploding inside his head.

Then he heard them laugh mockingly. The man who had kicked him said something he didn't entirely catch, but one word came through clearly: "Boy."

Boy. Mickey tensed like an overwound watch, so much he could hardly breathe. *Boy.* With a surge of effort, he did breathe, and, squeezing the knife so hard that it hurt his hand, he made a deft move upward and came to his feet more swiftly even than he had thought he could. His two antagonists backstepped clumsily, surprised by this move.

They were more surprised yet when Sparks made a graceful wheeling turn, thrusting out the knife at the same time. He aimed and swung hard, and the blade sliced first one throat, then a second, and the two Ellison men collapsed in bleeding heaps, terrible, gurgling, wheezing noises coming from them, hands gripping at sodden red throats.

"A boy, am I?" Sparks heard himself say. "Do those cut throats feel like the work of a boy, gentlemen? Or of a man?"

They could not have answered him if they'd wished to. They writhed and blubbered and bled, then slowly stopped moving. Sparks watched as the pair of them died before his eyes.

He shook his head slowly, feeling detached from it all. "Not a boy . . . not me. I ain't been a boy for a long time now."

He cleaned his knife on the shirt of one of the dead men and, before he lost his nerve, went to the door and out. He ran across the enclosure toward the big officer's house that was now the home of Bret Ellison.

He was not certain exactly how he would do what he had to do, but one thing he vowed: He would not leave this place until Bret Ellison was dead. Ellison could not be allowed to continue his course and kill Patrick Carrigan.

No. Killing Patrick Carrigan was a task that

Sparks would allow to be done by no one, except himself. He had his own balances to set right, and he'd come a long way to do that.

He was nearly to the house when he heard a noise in the shadows and turned quickly.

Someone was there. Someone had seen him leave the tack shed and was following.

CHAPTER THIRTEEN

"Patrick, this should be my task, not yours," Liam argued again as he and his uncle rode within sight of Ellison's stockade. "You cannot go in there and hope to come out again."

"But I do. Perhaps it's a vain hope, but I believe that Bret might at least be persuaded to spare my life. Especially given that I am handing myself to him freely. This is the last thing he would ever expect from me."

"I don't have your confidence in that regard. I believe we have no grounds for any kind of optimism. Joseph was a fool to come here, and we are fools, too, if we think that openly entering his own lair will result in anything but us being made his prisoners . . . or his victims. Especially you, whom he hates so badly."

"You may be right, but how can I, as a man of good character, stand by and allow my own nephew to receive ill treatment, or worse, in my place? Joseph is in there, still alive, God willing. But certainly in great danger. I must offer myself in return for his freedom."

"Please tell me why Ellison hates you so. I think I have a right to know."

Patrick paused for a long time. "Bret Ellison considers me the murderer of his wife. He has not forgiven me and probably cannot forgive me or believe that the act was anything but murder."

"Did you kill her?"

"I did, Liam. And killed part of my own soul when I did it. I had loved her, too, you see. Bret and I had vied for her, and he won the contest. No doubt, he believes it was jealousy and bitterness on my part that led me to kill her. But it was not. Not at all. It was self-defense."

"Tell me what happened."

Patrick looked at his nephew and seemed reluctant to continue. "If I go on, I'll be telling you things I never told my own son. I'll be revealing parts of my past that I wish were not there and that I could forget."

"Please, do tell me, though. I want to know why my brother is in danger right now and why I may be in danger myself within a few minutes."

The pair of them dismounted and knelt beside their horses in the same dark place where Mickey Sparks had, unknown to them, been present not very much earlier. They were unaware of Sparks's horse still tied behind a tree a hundred feet from them, where Sparks had left it before advancing on foot to the stockade.

"Joseph, I'll confess to you that when I was a young man, I made many bad choices and did many wrong things. Among the worst of them is that I took part in the robbery of a small bank in Missouri. With me at that time was another young man, my closest friend, Bret Ellison. He'd just won a battle with me for the heart of a beautiful young Missouri girl named Ann, daughter of a well-off farmer and livestock trader. Despite what I admit was great heartache and jealousy over Ann, I went through with the bank robbery with Bret. And we succeeded in taking several thousand dollars out of that bank, the deal being that we would split it between us evenly. But something happened to me in the meantime. Something called conscience. Your father and I were raised to be honest, God-fearing men, as I'm sure you know, Liam."

"Yes. Father raised Joseph and me the same way."

"I would expect he would do that. I had possession of the money from the robbery—all of it, because we hadn't yet divided it—and all the honest raising I'd received came to bear on me, Liam. I realized I—we—had done a very shameful, wrong thing. And I couldn't stand to go on with it. I decided to return the stolen money, anonymously, in a way that would not betray us as the robbers . . . and I made the mistake of telling Bret and Ann of my intentions.

"Bret didn't react too strongly to my plan—he had no real need of the money and had led the robbery for the pure excitement of doing it, I believe—but Ann held a far stronger view. She grew very angry, determined that I would not return that money, and, unknown to me, she followed me, found where I had hidden the money, and confronted me with a shotgun. She was going to take that money, all of it, for herself, and it was equally clear that she did not intend to leave me alive to betray her. I was stunned beyond all telling to know that she was capable of such evil. Remember, this was a young woman with whom I was much in love—as much as Bret was, I believe. But she forced me to defend my life against her. I had to shoot her, Liam. It was her life or mine. So I shot, and she died. And Bret Ellison came to hate me, and swore that someday he would take my life in return for Ann's. And what may sound strange to you is that I understood his feeling and half believed I deserved to be hated for what I'd done. The years have given me time to realize that what I did had to be done. It truly was self-defense. Ann truly would have killed me. For the sake of keeping stolen money, she would have killed me."

"And that is what is behind the War at Fire Creek? An old bank robbery and killing?"

"That's it, Liam. That's why all this hatred goes on, why two ranch foremen killed each other on the road today and two groups of cowboys shot at each other like opposing armies. Absurd, isn't it? An old sin just rolls up through the years and causes all this violence and hatred. And my own men are shot at and forced to act as protectors and soldiers—and that is not why I pay my men, Liam. I pay them to work for me, not to fight and die for me. This has to end. And it can only end at the hands of the same two men whose hands started it: Bret Ellison and me."

"You'll not do it alone, Patrick. I'll go in with you. But how can we enter? The gate is closed."

"All we need do is make our presence known," Patrick said. "If Bret knows his old enemy is out here seeking entrance, entrance we'll gain."

"Patrick, is there any chance at all that he'll listen to you and bring this to a peaceful conclusion? You could tell him of your regrets over what happened. Maybe that would soothe him."

"I cannot tell him that I was in the wrong, because I wasn't. But I can tell him my regrets, because there are plenty of them. Most of all, I regret having had to kill Ann, of all people, because of stolen bank money. God, what an absurd exchange for a life. What foolish people we were!"

"He may not listen to you at all, Patrick."

"Yes . . . he may kill me."

"If he does, he'll have to go through me to do it."

"He would not hesitate to do that."

"No, but he might find that getting past Liam Carrigan is not an easy thing to do."

"Don't get yourself killed to protect me, Liam. It wouldn't stop him—and the truth is, I am not worth it."

They decided to go forward on foot to the stockade, which left them with the problem of what to do with their horses. Liam, spotting a grove of trees, suggested they tie them there in hope of returning to fetch them later. Patrick agreed, and they led their horses over, by chance, to the same place where Mickey Sparks had left his horse earlier.

"Whose horse is this?" Patrick asked.

"It's Mickey's," said Liam. "I recognize it. This horse belongs to Mickey Sparks."

"Why is it here?"

"I don't know. Maybe Joseph rode it here instead of his own."

"Or perhaps Sparks followed him. Not that his name really is Sparks."

Liam frowned. "What do you mean, his name isn't Sparks?"

Patrick said, "I knew from the moment I saw that

man that I'd seen him before, somewhere. I couldn't remember where, though, and I persuaded myself I was mistaking him for someone else. But today I realized again that I knew him, and this time I remembered where . . . and who he really is."

"What's his name?"

"I don't know his first name—perhaps it really is Mickey. But his last name isn't Sparks, it's Cobbs."

"Cobbs . . . but why would he claim a different name from his real one?"

"Generally, when a man changes his name, he is trying to hide his identity from the world or from some particular person. In this case, I think that person is me."

"Where did you know him before?"

"In Tennessee, near Memphis. I lived there, very briefly, while I was still young and working my way westward. And it was there I first encountered Cobbs and his family. It was years ago, and he was just a young fellow."

"What happened?"

"A bad thing . . . a very bad thing. Something that never should have happened at all. I'll tell you about it another time . . . maybe."

"Is Sparks—Cobbs—a danger to you, Patrick?"

"I'm beginning to think that it's my past that's a danger to me. It seems that I am pursued by it. Every place I turn, I see its shadows rising to engulf me."

"Come, Patrick. Let's go on and see if we can bring this affair to a conclusion."

"Yes, let's."

Joseph, numb with a sense of hopeless dread and unaccountably weary, was unaware of it as his head tipped down and his chin came to rest on the upper part of his breastbone. He made a faint, murmuring noise and lost perception of the room around him and the presence of Bret Ellison, who at the moment stood by his mantelpiece again, looking up in silence at the painted figure he very nearly worshiped. Joseph's breathing became steady and slow as he drifted deeper into slumber.

It seemed an hour but, in fact, was mere moments later when he heard a noise. A firm, fist-on-wood rapping that pierced the shell of sleep and set his mind to working again. Joseph opened his eyes a little, and though the room was only moderately lighted, the lamplight glow hammered his eyes with faint jolts of pain. He frowned and sat up and, to his surprise, found a quilt tucked around his shoulders. Ellison had actually covered him, to keep him from growing cold as he slept.

The rapping again, and Ellison turned, showing Joseph a face again stained by tears. Ellison quickly brushed the moisture from his face with the heel of his hand, then headed toward the door of the big chamber.

Whoever was out there hammered out another round of knocks before Ellison could reach the door. "I'm coming," he said loudly, reaching for the huge brass door handle. He opened the door, and a figure staggered in swiftly, stumbling and nearly falling. Joseph gasped and came out of his chair. The man who had just entered, a stranger to him, was bloody from his collar to his waist, the front of his shirt drenched in red, which also deeply stained the jacket he wore over it.

"Poole!" Ellison exclaimed. "Dear God, man, what happened to you?" Ellison caught a glimpse of Joseph in the corner of his eye and turned to him, his fleshy face growing pallid. "This is James Poole," he said to Joseph. "James has worked for me for ten years, a capable cattleman and a wise general assistant. And now he has been hurt. Poole, my friend, what has happened to you?"

"Stabbed, sir . . . stabbed," the man said.

"Dear Lord, Poole. Stabbed by whom?"

"A negro, sir . . . he had crept into the stockade somehow . . . he has murdered Cruz and Bosworth . . . cut their throats, sir, in the tack shed. I found them there after I saw him creep out and come toward the house . . . God, sir, I feel I might faint."

While he spoke, Poole had been struggling to

stand up. Ellison grasped him by one shoulder and one elbow, steadying him. But Poole's face was white as milk, and he looked like a man close to oblivion. "Sit down, Poole," said Ellison. "I'll fetch you some wine to fortify you, then bring a physician from town."

Poole blinked and nodded and sank heavily into a chair. He turned his head to one side and spat up a bit, a mixture of stomach contents and blood that stank in the air. "Rest yourself, Poole," Ellison said. "Don't try to talk."

"Wait," said Joseph, rising and coming toward the others. "I need to ask a question. This negro, Mr. Poole, was he strongly built? Well featured? One eye slightly larger than the other and his hair thick but close-cropped?"

"Yes, yes, sir. That was him."

"Could be any of a hundred different negroes," said Ellison.

"Did he have on a blue shirt? And trousers made of canvas cloth?" asked Joseph.

"Yes, yes indeed. And wore-out boots."

"And a belt buckle that is different from most?"

"Yes . . . yes . . . a belt buckle that was made, somehow, from a pistol grip. Not the full grip, no bone or wood or nothing, just the metal sort of skeleton part that's on the inside. I noticed it right as he pulled out that knife to cut me."

"Where did this happen?"

"Just outside the house, sir. I saw him come out of the tack shed, and I thought it queer that he was in there, was inside the stockade at all. I was near the tack shed when he came out, just walking across from having gone to the privy, you see, so I stuck my head inside that door and seen two men's bodies lying still on the floor. I nearly passed out cold right there, sir. But I shook that off and went in long enough to see that I knew who they were. Then I came out, looking for that negro, and saw him, dodging into the shadows over near the house. I went after him, couldn't find him, and then he came out of the dark with his knife. I saw that belt buckle glitter in the light from the window. Then I saw the knife. And after that . . . it was something I don't relish describing, I can tell you. I just tried to get away from him, and finally I did. He just went back into the dark again, and I came and commenced to hammering on the door."

"So he's still out there," said Ellison. He turned a fierce glare on Joseph. "And judging from your questions, Carrigan, you know this negro. And I'm willing to bet you brought him here."

"Don't make that bet, sir. I didn't bring him here. But I do think I know who he is, and I suspect he has followed me. Maybe wanting to protect me."

"Who is he?"

"From the description, I feel sure it is a man named Mickey Sparks. A newcomer here, like me and my brother. We met him, struck it off rather well with him. I think he must have seen me leave the Carrigan ranch and decided to come after me."

"And now this friend of yours has murdered two of my men—two good, loyal men, both of them."

"I don't know what happened or how. I had nothing to do with it, Mr. Ellison. If Mickey followed, he did it on his own, and if he killed anyone, I like to believe he did it because he believed he had to. Self-defense."

"Self-defense," repeated Ellison in a snide tone. "I've heard that excuse given before, my friend."

"I don't know what you mean."

"Patrick Carrigan tried to excuse his murder by calling it self-defense. A preposterous claim. Imagine a big, strong man and a gentle, small, delicate young woman . . . and he tries to say his murder of her was something he had to do to defend himself. God, it makes an even greater mockery of her death."

"I know nothing of what happened other than what you told me. And there are usually two sides to every story. I've heard only one."

Something changed in Ellison's face. Until now, he'd had a certain subtly accommodating quality, almost a softness underlying his domineering manner, but suddenly that was gone. "Damn you!" he growled at Joseph. "Damn you for leading trouble and danger to my doorstep! Damn you for defending a man who merits no defense, a murderer of innocent young women! Damn you for being a *Carrigan!*"

And from beneath the flap of his coat, he drew out a small revolver, lifted it, aimed it at Joseph, and thumbed back the hammer.

"Wait! No!" Joseph exclaimed. "Don't shoot!"

"I will. I'll simply rid myself of one more Carrigan before he can become a problem. I've got problem enough with your damned uncle!"

He fired, and Joseph cried out and fell back hard, landing upon and smashing a small table.

"Bret . . . look out!" exclaimed Poole.

Ellison wheeled, startled by the urgency in Poole's voice. Poole was pointing toward the door, which remained ajar. He had a look of pure dread on his pallid face.

Ellison sensed movement at the door and looked just in time to see a black man in a dark blue shirt burst in, drawing a pistol out of his holster as he entered.

"You shot him!" Sparks exclaimed, raising the pistol.

Ellison was faster. He thumbed his hammer again and fired once, then twice more. The first two shots missed, but the third hit Sparks in the torso and knocked him down and back. He tried to keep a grip on his own pistol, but deep weakness crawled through him, and the pistol dropped from his fingers. Sparks murmured a curse and closed his eyes as night came through the walls and ceiling and closed around him like a blinding cloud.

CHAPTER FOURTEEN

Despite their anticipation of simply riding up to the gate of the stockade and being granted admittance by some of Ellison's men who would know their boss would be eager to receive his old enemy into his own fold, Patrick and Liam reached the stockade gate without even being seen. Outside, they lingered and debated and at last decided simply to go over the wall.

Patrick, a strong and limber man for his age, went over first, boosted by Liam's strong arms. Liam had it harder, having to resort to finding footholds and grip points as Sparks had earlier. He reached the top of the stockade and dropped over inside, landing just beside his uncle.

"Dear God, the belly of the beast," he said, looking around.

"Indeed."

"What now? There are lights at Ellison's house."

"Not there, not yet. I want to think this out first."

Should we not have thought it out before we got this far? Liam thought, but without saying it aloud.

"There's a shed over there, with the door partly open," Liam said. "We can be out of view in there."

"Where do you think Mickey Cobbs is?" asked Patrick.

"I have no way to know. Come on . . . the shed. We can talk better in there, and no one will see us."

"Lead the way."

They had just found the bodies when they became conscious of motion and noise outside. Liam remained to stare at the corpses and try to figure out just what had happened to them and whether Joseph had anything to do with it. Patrick crept to the window of the shed, looked across at the house, and saw a dark form, possibly that of Mickey Cobbs, moving through a doorway into the Ellison residence. He was too far away to make out much detail or to be sure of exactly what he was seeing, but he had been told that Ellison made his principal quarters in a large room on the lowest floor. And through the little square of light created by the opening of the door, Patrick's sharp eyes had caught sight of a second figure already inside the room . . . and it looked like Ellison.

"Liam, I think I saw him."

"Who?"

"Ellison."

"Where?"

"Inside the house. A door opened. And I think Mickey Cobbs went inside."

"Where Ellison is?"

"Yes . . . same room."

Liam came up from the back of the shed and joined his uncle. "Those men have had their throats cut."

"Do you think it could have been Joseph?"

"I can't see Joseph cutting anyone's throat. More likely it was Sparks, or Cobbs, or whatever Mickey's name really is. Or maybe it was something completely unrelated. But they are sure enough dead."

And then they heard the shots from the house.

They looked at each other. "Let's go," Patrick said.

"Let's do."

Everything from that moment on became quite strange. Liam and Patrick left the shed and ventured daringly into the open. They darted straight toward the house, Patrick leading the way, and suddenly there were others around them, Ellison men drawn out of various places by the same gunshots the Carrigans had heard.

Liam braced himself for the moment one of them would recognize Patrick and react. Oddly, none of the Ellison men paid them any particular heed. They were simply two more figures among several others, and everyone's attention was on the house, everyone's mind on those shots.

The group reached the house, and one of the Ellison men burst right in, followed by several others. Liam and Patrick brought up the rear and found themselves forced merely to look inside, across the shoulders of those who had gone in before.

Liam, having never met Ellison, was not sure what or whom to look for, but it was easy to figure out who Ellison was from the manner in which he was addressed and treated. But Liam found the man only of limited interest, because his eye was locked on the body of his brother, lying on the floor in the midst of a ruined, smashed table. There was blood on his chest, but, thank God, the chest was moving with ragged breaths.

Liam did not hesitate but walked up through the group and past Ellison, who stared at him strangely because of his similarity to Patrick Carrigan, and knelt beside Joseph.

"He's shot!" Liam said, looking up at Ellison. "Who shot him?"

"Not sure," Ellison lied. "A pistol went off by accident when it got knocked off a shelf over there. He fell at the same time. I think that bullet was the one that got him."

Liam wasn't buying it, but now was not the time to beat that particular horse. He had to make sure

Joseph was not mortally hurt. He leaned over and spoke to Joseph, whose eyes were closed.

"Joseph, brother, wake up. Let me see you look back at me."

Joseph's eyes fluttered and opened; his lips parted in a little smile when he saw Liam looking down at him. "Ellison shot me," he said in a hoarse whisper.

"I figured. How bad off are you?"

"Weak . . . but I feel like I'll make it through. Hurts, though."

Liam glanced up and saw that the number of men in the room had diminished. Several of Ellison's men had withdrawn from the room. Liam wasn't sure what had drawn them out, but he suspected it might be that lack of personal dedication to Ellison's little war that had led Ellison's fighters to withdraw from the battle on the road earlier.

His gaze dropped, and he saw Mickey Sparks on the floor, blood on him. He was moving, apparently coming back to his senses after a faint. *Good Lord*, thought Liam. *Men with throats cut, others lying with bullets in them. What kind of place is this?*

Then Liam noticed Patrick. He was standing in the back of the room, facing a corner, looking as if he were merely reading the titles of books on a shelf. With his face not showing, his identity was not immediately obvious. A wise strategic move, Liam thought. Had Patrick's identity been noted immediately by the group as a whole, it was hard to guess what kind of response it might have generated among Ellison's men.

Ellison stepped in front of Liam, looking down at him. "You have to be the brother, and damned if you aren't like a picture image of the man I despise most in the world."

"So a lot of people have been telling me," Liam said, rising and looking Ellison in the eye. "My brother needs help. I want a doctor brought in here."

"Your brother brought danger to this place. He led this darky here," Ellison said, kicking at Mickey on the floor.

Mickey moved suddenly, reaching out and grabbing Ellison's ankle. He pulled, and Ellison lost his footing and fell, a heavy heap on the floor. Liam knelt beside him and jammed the muzzle of his pistol against Ellison's neck.

"This war between you and my uncle is over," he said. "You're going to call all your men off. You're going to tell them that there is no more harassment of Patrick Carrigan's men. And you're going to call off any attempt to kill my uncle. Is that clear?"

Ellison's face blanched, and he lost the ability to speak for a few moments. His eyes shifted, rolling around in his head as he looked for rescue. "Men . . . help me!" he called, risking a shot from Liam's pistol.

"Go ahead and yell," Liam said. "They're all gone,

Ellison. None of them in here to help you. They've all left the room. They're willing to herd cattle for you, maybe even to take a potshot or two at some of my uncle's cowboys, but now there are men starting to die, and their loyalty doesn't go that far. They're not going to die for a cause that isn't theirs."

"Can I sit up?" Elllison asked, seeming rather pitiful now.

"Go ahead."

Ellison sat up and looked around and saw for himself that he was alone and unprotected. Every one of his men who had been drawn by the earlier gunfire had left.

But there was one man remaining, standing at the back of the room, looking at books on a shelf. Ellison looked at him, then frowned. And Patrick Carrigan, perhaps feeling the eyes upon him, turned and looked Bret Ellison in the face.

The two enemies were without words for a full minute. They hardly blinked, simply locked gazes and held them. Ellison actually held his breath for about twenty seconds, not even aware he was doing it, then gasped explosively. Then he stared in silence awhile longer, breathing fast.

"You!" he said at last. "Damn your soul, Carrigan! How dare you set foot in this house! How dare you even come into the presence of her image?" He waved toward the portrait above the mantelpiece.

Patrick looked up at the image of beautiful Ann Ellison, and looked as if someone had just kicked him in the ribs. He winced, put the back of a hand over his mouth, and took two steps back, knocking off the shelf two or three of the books whose spines he'd been studying so intently moments before.

"Welcome to your death, Carrigan!" Ellison yelled at him. "You've walked into this room never to walk out again." He reached under his coat and drew out a derringer, which he raised and aimed at Patrick.

"Hell no!" yelled the wounded Mickey on the floor. He came up, pistol in hand, and shoved it against Ellison's back. Fresh blood began to pour from his wound again, but he ignored it. "Drop that little pistol, old man!" he ordered.

Ellison glanced at him, a hateful, burning glance, then aimed at Patrick's chest and pulled the trigger of the derringer. It misfired. Liam lifted his pistol, ready to shoot Ellison, but Mickey fired before he could do so. The bullet tore deeply into the rancher's body, and he fell at once, bleeding and moaning.

Patrick Carrigan had drawn his own pistol by that point, but he dropped it in shock as his enemy fell. He walked over and knelt beside Ellison, leaning over him and holding his head in his hands.

"Bret . . . Bret, don't die. Don't die."

"Don't . . . touch . . . me . . ."

"Bret, we were friends once, you and me. Just

young, foolish men but friends. Let's not let it end like this, not hating each other."

"I do . . . hate you . . . I must . . . because of . . . her." Ellison's eyes shifted toward the portrait.

Patrick looked up at the picture, tears coming into his eyes. "She tried to kill me, Bret. She didn't want me to give the money back to the bank. She threatened to shoot me, and I had to shoot her first."

"You . . . murdered her."

"I made many mistakes in my life when I was young, Bret. But I've never murdered anyone. I didn't murder Ann. I killed her, but it was not murder. It was self-defense."

"I'll see you . . . in hell, Patrick."

Ellison squeezed his eyes shut and bit his lip. His body shuddered and then relaxed. With his head still held by the man he'd hated so long, he died beneath the unseeing gaze of the portrait on the wall above the fireplace.

"God help me . . . he's gone," Patrick said. "Bret is gone."

Liam examined Ellison closely. "Yes. He is gone. He's dead, Uncle Patrick. You're safe now."

"No," said Mickey, still on his feet despite his wound. "Not safe. I'm going to kill you, Patrick Carrigan. I came many miles to do it."

Liam looked up at Mickey and was stunned to see his pistol aimed at Patrick Carrigan's head. "I killed your enemy, but that was only so I'd be the one who gets to kill you. I owe you, Irishman. I owe you because of my father, George."

"Drop the pistol, Mickey, or I'll kill you right here," Liam said, aiming his own pistol at Mickey's head.

Mickey's response was swift and wordless. He simply turned his pistol on Liam and fired. The shot was poorly aimed and caught Liam in the shoulder, but it numbed and weakened his arm and caused him to drop his pistol. Joseph, still on the floor, reached for the fallen pistol, but Mickey aimed at him and made him stop, then collected the pistol himself. He tossed it out the door into the darkness.

"Why, Mickey?" Liam asked, gripping his bleeding shoulder. "Why do you want to kill my uncle?"

"I can tell you that," Patrick said. "He wants to kill me because he believes I helped kill his father years ago, in the western end of Tennessee."

"That's right," Mickey said. "George Cobbs. Just a hardworking sharecrop farmer. Falsely accused of hurting a white woman. And a bunch of brave men hiding behind white bedsheets came around one night and took him out of his own house and hauled him off in the woods and put a rope around his neck." Mickey snarled at Patrick. "One of them was you, Patrick Carrigan. For I saw you with my own eyes, after it was over. You standing there with that damned white robe in your hand, you staring up at my father's face while he hung there dead."

"You did see that, Mickey. But you didn't see what you thought you did. I was there, but that white robe wasn't mine. It belonged to the only one of the lynch mob I was able to persuade not to take part in that lynching. For that's what I did that night, Mickey. I didn't help with the hanging, I tried to stop it."

"A damned liar you are! And I'll kill you this night."

"You're already shot, Mickey. You're still losing blood," Liam said. "Drop that pistol, and let us get you help, before you die right there on your feet."

"I'll not die . . . not until I see him die first. It was hard to track you down, Patrick Carrigan. Harder than any of the others. And I tracked every one of them, all over this country. And I killed them all, one by one. You're the last. And tonight is your night."

"I didn't help hang your father, Mickey. And when I failed to stop that hanging, I took it on myself to try to help your family. You remember that butchered hog that your mother found in the back of your wagon three months after you lost your father? Your family lived on that meat all winter. I put that hog there, Mickey. I bought it and had it butchered and put it there. And you remember the rifle that was left on your doorstep with your brother's name on it? I put it there. I gave it to him because I knew he needed it for hunting. And the money your mother received in the mail from time to time—that was money I earned and mailed to her. Long as she lived."

Mickey's hand trembled; it was hard for him to hold up the pistol now. "How you know about them things?"

"Because I'm the one who did them. And I wouldn't know about them otherwise, would I? Think about it, Mickey. Don't shoot me. If you do, you'll be shooting the man who tried to save your father's life and who helped support your family for years thereafter."

"I don't know if I can believe you."

"It's true, Mickey. I vow before God." He looked down at Ellison. "There's been enough people die here tonight. Let's end it now. Please, put down the pistol."

Mickey Cobbs lowered the pistol, then laid it on a chair. He looked weak and sick. Liam went to his side and helped him ease down onto a sofa. Cobbs closed his eyes, and his breathing faltered but did not stop.

"Uncle Patrick," Liam said, "I suggest we get out of this stockade as quickly as we can and get all these wounded folks to a doctor."

"A good suggestion, Liam Carrigan," Patrick said. "Come . . . I don't think anyone will try to stop us. Ellison's men have already proven their level of disloyalty by abandoning him when he needed him most. Let's go."

* * *

Liam carressed Allie's hand and smiled into her pretty face, the taste of her kiss fresh on his lips.

"It was worth traveling all the way to Montana just to meet you, Allie," he said. "I know I'm older than you are, but I swear, I believe you're the very woman I could find myself unable to live without. Just like Joseph and Charlotte. They've already got a date set, and it's only been six months since we got here."

"It's a lot different now than when you came," Allie said.

"That's true. Thank God that war is over. Six months of peace, no cowboys shooting at one another, Patrick not having to hide out anymore."

"And you only saw the last two or three days of the war," she said. "It had been going on a good while longer before you got here."

"I know. Glad we missed it."

"I'm glad you came, not only because of getting to know you and love you, but because you and Joseph brought peace with you. You ended the war."

"The truth is, Mickey Cobbs ended the war when he killed Bret Ellison. Though it's too bad that had to happen. It would have been best to see him and Patrick make peace, if that was possible."

"I don't think it was."

"You're probably right."

"Where is Mickey now? I wish he'd stayed on to work longer. He was a good cowboy."

"Yes, but I think that every time he saw Patrick, he was reminded of the mistake he made and how he might have killed a man who helped his family survive after his father died. Dear Lord, what a past Patrick has had!"

"His future will be better. Thanks to you and Joseph. I'm so glad that Joseph's wounds healed so well."

"So am I. I'd hate to lose that brother of mine, irritating as he can be. I guess I love the man. And I love you, too, Allie."

"I love you, Liam. Forever."

"That's a long time."

"Then let's live it together."

He smiled and kissed her again. Taking her hand, he walked beside her toward the Carrigan house. It was suppertime, and the scent of stewed beef filled the ranch grounds.

They went inside together and joined Joseph, Patrick, and Charlotte Canaday at the big table, heavily laden with food. It was a beautiful night, cool and clear and full of peace.

ROUND 'EM UP!

THE BEST IN WESTERNS FROM POCKET STAR BOOKS

Cameron Judd
The Carrigan Brothers series
Shootout in Dodge City
Revenge on Shadow Trail

Cotton Smith
The Texas Ranger series
The Thirteenth Bullet

Gary Svee
Spur Award-winning author
The Peacemaker's Vengeance
Spirit Wolf
Showdown at Buffalo Jump
Sanctuary

Jake Lancer
Golden Spike Trilogy
Big Iron

Dusty Richards
The Marshal Burt Green series
Deuces Wild